"Do you want to feel, or do you want to forget?"

Kentucky's touch was still soothing, but it made Sean burn hotter, too. "Because after the orgasm is over, you realize those things you were hiding from never left."

"Wasn't this what you wanted when you brought me out here?" He lifted his head and met her eyes. "If it's not, tell me to stop and we'll forget this ever happened."

Her eyes were luminous and open. She wanted him, but she wanted more than what he was offering her.

"I don't want to forget it happened, and I especially don't want you to forget I happened."

He pushed her down in the sand and pressed her beneath him. Color was high in her cheeks and her eyes glittered in the firelight. Her arms twined around his neck. She obviously didn't give a damn they were out in the open, with her hair fanned out in the sand.

"Live a little." His mouth descended toward hers oh-so-slowly...

Dear Reader,

I hope you enjoy reading about Sean and Kentucky. Like all my characters, they're dear to my heart and their road to happily-ever-after is a bumpy one. But isn't that what makes it so worth it? It makes the light at the end of the darkness so much brighter and that much warmer.

Wishing you your own happily-ever-after, and with much love,

Sara Arden

Sara Arden

No Surrender

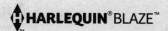

Recycling programs
for this product may
not exist in your area.

ISBN-13: 978-0-373-79906-0

No Surrender

Copyright © 2016 by Sara Lunsford

This edition published by arrangement with Harlequin Books S.A.

For questions and comments about the quality of this book, please contact us at CustomerService@Harlequin.com.

Printed in U.S.A.

Sara Arden lives in a small Kansas town with her husband, two children, a horse, two cats and a bunny. She started reading romance at a young age, and by the time she entered high school, aced world history without ever cracking her textbook because of all the historicals she'd read. Besides reading, Sara enjoys travel, the smell of old books, tea and pedicures. She loves to hear from her readers.

For the babybats

Prologue

KENTUCKY LEE MUTTERED under her breath as she watched a sniping pack of carnivorous prowling she-wolves gather around the newly single Special Operations pilot, Sean Dryden. She knew what they were all thinking as they dabbed artfully at their conveniently waterproof eyeliner and made the appropriate sounds of condolence and grief. All talking about what a shame it was that Lynnie James was gone.

She knew each one of them wondered how soon was too soon to offer him comfort of another sort in hopes of catching him like a rabbit in a trap. They were all plotting against one other like corrupt Roman senators.

It wasn't a surprise that anyone would want him. He was, in a word, beautiful. He was all-American Boy Scout perfection. Kentucky didn't blame them for being attracted to him. Sean Dryden was everyone's type. Kentucky could only hope none of them would be stupid enough to make a move here. Especially where she could see. Kentucky would end up a headline in the town rag for causing a scene at the James funeral.

Lynnie James had been her best friend and Sean's fiancée. This potluck in the Saint Paul Lutheran Church basement consisting of fallout-shelter green-bean casserole, macaroni slathered in "processed cheese food" and bacon bits like gravel was all in her honor. Which was rather kind of terrible. Kentucky hoped that when she left this world, people would do something more interesting, something that reflected the person she was.

Green-bean casserole didn't begin to sum up the beautiful soul that was Lynnie James. No one really could.

Kentucky didn't begrudge them their grieving rituals or their terrible choices of potluck dishes. It was just that she didn't belong. She never had. While the others could hug each other, remember the good times with the all-American girl who made life in small-town Winchester, Kansas, worth living, Kentucky didn't have that.

Not with anyone but Lynnie.

Her best friend had been the only one who really saw her. Not just the party girl who liked fast boys and faster cars—the rebel without a cause. Lynnie had seen everything—the good, the bad, the ugly—and loved her unconditionally. Lynnie had always been on her side.

Kentucky missed her for all those reasons and more.

She caught Sean's eye and watched as he extracted himself from the fray of she-wolves and headed straight for her. She could feel the women glaring hot enough to burn through to her bones. But that was the same way they'd looked at her in high school. It bothered her even less now than it did then. She knew who she was, knew her own worth.

He embraced her. "You look beautiful. I never thought I'd see you in a dress."

She was suddenly aware of the black dress, the way it clung to her, and the knowledge that Sean's eyes had been on her and liked it. She flushed, her face hot. Kentucky hated that she had this reaction. She felt like a first-class traitor having this reaction to Sean, here of all places.

"Well, it is Lynnie's funeral. What else would I do?" She fumbled with her hands and then smoothed them down the sides of her dress. It was too tight, a lace prison that caged her breath so she could inhale only shallowly.

His brown eyes were full of some emotion that was more than grief but that she couldn't name. "You know Lynnie wouldn't have cared what you wore."

It was then with the sadness etched on his face that she realized what was in the depths of his eyes: guilt. "Sean, what happened—" she paused, searching for the right thing to say "—it wasn't your fault. The roads were icy. There's nothing that you could've done. It was black ice."

He looked away from her and for a moment it seemed as if he'd frozen in place. Then when he met her gaze again, she saw so much pain it was suffocating. "There's so much you don't know."

She reached out and grabbed his shoulders. "I know all I need to know. I know that Lynnie loved you and I know that you loved her. That's all that matters."

She hated being here, enduring other people and their grief. Not Sean so much as the acquaintances who didn't really know Lynnie. The acquaintances who knew only Lynnie James the former cheerleader who was going to be a kindergarten teacher and marry her high school sweetheart.

How Kentucky's heart hurt for him. He seemed so lost, so broken and oh-so alone. She hugged him again. She wanted him to know that he wasn't alone. He didn't have to be lost. The gesture was meant to be comforting, and she couldn't help but feel guilty for enjoying the sensation of being locked in his arms for just a moment.

She was supposed to be offering him support, but she took strength and safety from his embrace. It reminded her that even though Lynnie was gone, she wasn't alone. Or maybe they were just alone together.

"She loved you, too, Kentucky. So much that I know she wouldn't want you to stay here. She'd know you were ready to jump out of your own skin. She'd tell you to run and she'd probably even cover for you." He released her from the hug and she reluctantly stepped back from him.

Lynnie had known her inside and out. She'd been the best of friends. Hell, how she missed her. Kentucky smiled softly. "But funerals aren't really for the dead, though, are they? They're for the living." She looked at him pointedly.

"You don't have to stay for me." Sean scrubbed a hand over his face. "The sooner I can get out of here, the better. It's just too much, you know?"

"Yeah." She nodded. "I get it. I really do."

Sean studied her for a moment. "I know you do."

He grabbed her and hugged her again, but this time it was hard and quick. "You meant the world to Lynnie." He released her. "And you mean a lot to me. Don't be a stranger."

1

BUT THAT WAS exactly what she was: a stranger.

Kentucky didn't see or hear anything from Sean Dryden until July, seven months after they said goodbye to the woman they loved.

He'd gone back to his assignment and didn't email or answer her letters. Not even when she sent him the little notebook of poetry Lynnie had written about him in middle school.

She didn't know what she expected from him. What was there to say?

Kentucky hoped he was okay, he was safe, and he was processing as best he could. Most important, she hoped he'd realized that Lynnie's death wasn't his fault.

She thought about them a lot. The group, the way they used to be. Herself, Lynnie, Sean, Eric and Rachel. But now Lynnie's brother, Eric, was with Rachel. That wasn't really a surprise either. They'd been best friends since they were in diapers. It was kind of a natural progression.

Kentucky was happy for them, but there was still an empty place inside her where Lynnie used to be.

And Sean, God, Sean.

She shook her head at her own train of thought, as if that would shake him out of the spot he occupied in her brain. He didn't belong there, never had. Yet still, he had his own room in her head. He always had. She'd never wanted to take anything from Lynnie, but she couldn't help the way she wanted Sean Dryden.

She'd dreamed about him the way little girls do members of boy bands. Until it had turned to something earthier in her teens. Something more carnal. He had been her ultimate fantasy. She'd played scenarios out in her head all the time then. Scenarios that involved meeting him under the bleachers after football practice to make out. Or playing Seven in Heaven or Truth or Dare at some party. But Seven in Heaven had been her favorite for a while. If they were locked in the dark together for seven minutes, they were expected to make out. He'd kiss her, touch her, and she'd get to touch him and it would all be okay because it was just a game.

She'd even dreamed that Lynnie would break it off with him and he'd come to her for solace. Sometimes that one made her hate herself because she was wishing to break something that could never be broken or *should* never be broken for her own gain.

Kentucky rationalized it by saying that it was only in her head. She never acted on it. Never actively wished for bad things. It was more of a passive sort of wishing. Not that it was any better, but it helped her sleep at night in those first years, when she'd wanted him so much she could taste it.

When they'd gotten engaged, Lynnie and Sean, she'd known the rightness of it. Accepted it. She'd managed to stop thinking about him every day. But sometimes she still felt that familiar tug in her belly, the tingle between her legs when his hand would brush hers, or she could feel the heat of his body when he sat next to her.

She knew it was pathetic, but that didn't stop her.

Now Lynnie was gone, and in a way, she guessed Sean was, too.

It was late on a sticky July afternoon when Kentucky Lee was sure the moonshine cherries she'd been eating while hanging out on the deck of the Shooting Star Honky-Tonk had conjured a ghost.

Sean Dryden, looking as hollow and broken as he had the day of Lynnie's funeral, sat down in the chair next to her. Its old rusted metal base creaked under his weight, but he didn't seem to notice. A day's growth of beard shadowed his handsome face. He had a bottle of her locally sourced—homemade—shine in his hand.

He looked like hell.

And still, he was the handsomest man she'd ever seen in real life.

She offered him a cherry and he offered her a sip of shine.

"I didn't think that was your speed." Kentucky pointed her chin at the moonshine.

"It's not really, but it's good for what ails you. Isn't that what your grandmother used to say?"

"She sure did." Kentucky nodded.

"I like that about you."

"What?" She looked up.

"No small talk. No accusations wondering why I'm not out playing flyboy." He said this last bit derisively.

"Playing flyboy? I think what you do is a little more important than that." As a special ops pilot, it was his job to get operatives in and out of war zones. To move undetected through enemy airspace and ensure the safety of his team and everyone aboard his Black Hawk.

And to destroy whatever operational targets had been provided.

"That's just it. You're the only one."

"I'm sure that's not the case." Everyone was mostly in awe of what he did, at least the parts he could tell people about.

"You'd be surprised."

At the expression on his face, she was reminded of the day of the funeral and all the she-wolves looking to take him down like prey. "So why are you home?"

He wrinkled his nose. "Mental health days."

"You only got a few days before. It was inhumane. I'm glad you got some more time." There was no way he could've been expected to deal with his loss in the week he'd been given at home before he'd had to return to duty.

"I'd have rather spent it on a beach somewhere. That would be some real mental health recuperation." He took another swig of shine.

He was so hard, so angry. She couldn't blame him for it either. Kentucky knew she would be, too.

They passed the bottle back and forth between them

a couple of times and sat in a companionable silence
for a long moment.

She tried not to think about the heat that burned her
fingers when their hands brushed as he handed her the
bottle. Or that his firm mouth had been where her lips
were, that it was almost like a kiss. It was the closest
she'd ever get to something like that with a guy like him.

Guilt surged and washed over her desire, tamping
it down to some small, inconsequential thing. But the
flame still burned, flickered like a newly lit candle.
Kentucky exhaled heavily.

"I just can't do it." He tossed back some more moonshine. "It's stifling here."

She turned to look at him. The chiseled ridge of his
clenched jaw, the stiff set to his broad shoulders, the
tension that thrummed through him like a live wire.
Kentucky wished she could ease his pain.

And her own.

"I know, right?" She pursed her lips. "I've never been
like them. Like you."

"Me?" Sean pushed the bottle toward her. "What
does that mean?"

"You know, the kind who fits in." She shrugged.

"You fit in more than you know. You don't have to
hide who you are to be special, Kentucky."

Part of her wanted to argue with him, to deny any
of the more tender things that could hurt her. But this
had been part of her fantasies. That he always knew
who she was.

And wanted her anyway.

She swallowed. "Yeah, well, you know." Great.

That sentence didn't even make any sense. Kentucky shrugged again. "I can do that, too. Shine a light on things you'd rather not see. Like Lynnie's death." She fixed him with a hard stare. "It wasn't your fault."

He looked away from her. "Yes, it was. There are things you don't know, Kentucky."

"Like what? Like you made the road slick? You made her brakes fail? It was a terrible accident that could've happened to any of us." Of course he felt guilty because he hadn't been here. Logic wouldn't fix that for him. Only he could make it right in his own head.

"I can't talk about it." His stare was focused somewhere out on the horizon. Somewhere he could be that wasn't here, in this place, without Lynnie. Or that was what she imagined.

She pursed her lips again, feeling them go tight and thin. "You don't have to. I think I've had enough of talking. At least talking about death. Because we're still here. We're still alive."

"Are you sure about that?"

Kentucky mustered up a grin. "I guess I don't know about you, but *I* am." This was what she'd been waiting for. Some grand spark of inspiration, a way to honor Lynnie's life that represented who she was. Not the Saint Paul Lutheran Ladies Auxiliary version. Lynnie had always been so vital. Her life was like a star, something bright and sparkling.

"Come on." She held out her hand as she stood. "Let's get out of here."

Sean cocked his head to the side and seemed to debate for a long moment. "Screw it." He took her hand and hopped up to his feet. "Where are we going?"

"Come with me and find out." She dragged him behind her toward the back of the property, his warm fingers closed around hers.

She wouldn't think about how good it felt to hold his hand, to have some solid anchor keeping her in the moment. As she drew him deeper into the wooded area, he paused.

"Mossy Rock? You can't be serious."

"I'm so serious right now." She tugged his hand and he followed. "Lynnie loved it out here. Do you remember?"

"Yeah." His voice was tight with emotion.

Mossy Rock was a place right out of a teen drama. It was the weekend place for Winchester teens in the summer and early fall before the air turned cold and sharp. Mossy Rock was like a backwoods waterslide right into Sutter's Pond.

It was known for camping, the occasional kegger, bonfires and long summer days spent in the water floating around on inner tubes and sunning on the grass around the pond.

She stopped just at the edge of the rock. "Are you in?"

"I'm not sliding down that rock, Kentucky." His voice sounded like some sitcom dad, faux stern.

"Then I guess I'm going to leave you here by yourself. Sucks for you." She pulled off her boots and arched a brow. Kentucky knew that all she had to do was basically dare him to do it and he'd be in the water right after her.

"Not going to happen."

"Chicken." She started peeling off her jeans. She tried not to think about her bare legs or to wonder if he'd look, wonder if she wanted him to look.

Or what he'd look like naked.

"I'm not going to do something just because you— What are you doing?" He watched her slide the denim down her legs and her face heated.

"What, did you think I was going to slide down that rock in my clothes? No way." She'd be in nothing but her underwear. She rationalized that it was the same as wearing a bikini. Nothing less was covered.

He chuckled. "You're still that same wild creature you've always been."

She met his gaze. "Always and forever." Kentucky meant to sound lighthearted, but it ended up sounding more like a confession. But that wasn't anything he didn't already know. "And I'm not the only one. You may be a Boy Scout, Sean Dryden, but you don't get to be a special ops pilot by sitting on the sidelines." She knew that spark was still in him, that fire. It just needed to be rekindled.

"Next you're going to say to live a little. Am I right?" He shook his head. "Hell, I think you said those exact words to me last time we were all here." Sean pointed to the top of Mossy Rock. "It was me, you, Lynnie, Eric and Rachel the weekend before graduation. I still hadn't decided if I was going to K-State or enlisting."

She smiled at him. "And Lynnie said you were her hero no matter what you chose."

Shadows of emotion fell across his face. "But you, you told me live a little."

"And are you?" Had he really enlisted because she'd told him to? That was insane. No one made life choices on an offhand comment made by the one in the group most likely to leave a good-looking corpse.

"I think I meant to," Sean answered.

"So what are you doing? Come on." She pulled her shirt off and slid down Mossy Rock into Sutter's Pond. Things were getting too heavy again, too hot. Kentucky was intently aware of his eyes and everything his gaze touched. Like the sun stretching out rays of heat all down her skin.

She squeaked as the cool water enveloped her and she stayed beneath the dark surface for a time, the moment frozen, her feelings frozen. Under the water, she didn't have to think about losing Lynnie.

Under the water, she didn't have to think about Sean.

All she had to do was float. The weight of the water both pushed her down and held her suspended at the same time, or so it seemed to her. It was this strange sensation of nonbeing. But she only stayed there like a movie on pause. She didn't want to stop feeling; she didn't want to be frozen forever. She wanted a second where she didn't have to do anything but float; then she could hit Play on the world again.

She let everything crash back into her as she surfaced. Her loss, her need, her desire and her hope. Her hope that she could cram everything she wanted to feel and experience into this life. It was over much too quickly, like fireworks.

He splashed into the water behind her.

Why had she thought this was a good idea again? Kentucky had only wanted to take his mind off their pain. But her mind was on something else altogether. She turned around to face him and he stood there bare chested like a freshwater Poseidon.

Sean scrubbed his hand over his face and pushed away the droplets of water. He grinned. His biceps bulged, the veins in his forearms raised under his tanned skin. She wanted to touch it, trace those lines up his arm, close her hands around his shoulders and pull him down to— She wouldn't think about that now. She'd let herself have that fantasy when she was alone in the dark and pretending her own fingers were his.

She wouldn't think about standing there in her wet bra and panties or the way the water slid down over the hard lines of his face, the sheen of water on his skin or the fact that he was wearing nothing but his issued boxer briefs, which molded to his body... Nope. Wasn't going to think about it at all. Or the way he seemed to be looking at the lace that cupped her breasts. This could only lead to regret.

Not for her, but for him. He was hurting now and looking for something to stanch the pain. What better way than to get lost in another person? Her skin, her touch, her scent...that contact pushing away all the darkness, quieting the sadness, if only for a time.

But he'd feel guilty for it later—she knew that.

But if he kept looking at her that way, she was going

to take him up on it. She'd wanted him for so long, and she didn't do things like regret. Life was too fleeting. They were both still breathing and as much as she loved Lynnie, she was gone and she wasn't coming back.

Instead of facing the burn growing between them, she splashed him.

His eyes narrowed and he pounced, catching her easily. He hoisted her high in the air and tossed her. She gave a small squeal of protest, but she loved it. The feeling of flying, no matter how brief, was amazing.

She came up from the water, elated and laughing. "So that's all it takes, huh? Did you forget I love that?"

"No, I didn't forget." He snatched her up again, his broad, strong fingers scorching where they touched.

Kentucky rested her palms on his shoulders, unable and unwilling to fight the heady rush that came from both his nearness and the thrill she got from being flung through the air.

He threw her easily and she laughed again before splashing down into the water.

Sean tossed her a few more times and they swam in the little pond until dusk fell and Kentucky began to shiver. But she didn't want to stop; she didn't want this to be over.

Even though the fact that it had to end made it more special somehow.

Her teeth chattered as the night air blew brisk on her wet flesh, but she could shiver and chatter later. When Sean and these moments were gone.

"That's it for you, Kentucky. You're going to catch cold. Out of the water."

"You're not the boss of me," she teased, and stuck her tongue out.

"As if, woman." He shook his head. "No one is the boss of you. Never has been, never will be. But—" he eyed her "—I am someone who cares about you and wants you to take care of yourself."

She opened her mouth and snapped it shut again, chattering aside. Kentucky really couldn't argue with that. It was one of the things she adored about Sean. Lynnie's brother, Eric, had always been the "do as I say" "I'm in charge" sort. He had the same motivation for looking out for their group, because he cared. But Sean didn't have to stamp his say-so on everything. He didn't try to make her do anything, even if he thought it was best.

He never tried to crush the wild out of her.

"I suppose you could entice me with a fire." She nodded to the makeshift fire pit that had been dug next to the pond.

"Hmm. I suppose I could if I knew how to start a fire." He made a big show of shrugging his massive shoulders as if he were somehow helpless.

"Oh, please. You could start a fire with a piece of bark and a shoelace. Don't be demure now."

"Maybe I just want to see how long you'll stay in the water to spite me." He climbed out of the pond and headed toward the pit.

She laughed. "It's not to spite you. If I stay covered, I'm warmer."

"You'd be warmer over here. Next to me."

She shivered again, but this time it wasn't from the

cold. Anticipation of what it could mean to share body heat with him, to be pressed up against his firm body...

"Come on, stubborn."

Kentucky realized she was still standing in the water, staring at him, and he'd already built a small fire.

She bit her lip, indecision holding her back. Kentucky knew what she wanted, but did she want it enough to trade her friendship with him? They were both hurting and anyone who didn't know where this little vignette by a fire under the stars would lead was kidding themselves.

Or naive.

They were both more worldly than that.

Kentucky had always been one to throw the cards up in the air and let them land where they may.

Maybe she was wrong about how Sean would feel. She'd just acknowledged they both knew how things worked. Maybe he'd take comfort in her and her in him and they could let it be just that.

She crept up out of the water and sat down on the sand next to him. She remembered how they'd all chipped in from their summer jobs to buy the sand to spread so they could have the fire pit. It was the old farmer's one caveat to letting the kids stay on his property. Mossy Rock didn't technically belong to him, but no one in Winchester County was going to tell him that.

His arm slid around her and he pulled her down with him. She settled against him, memorizing where their bodies touched and how the heat contrasted with the night air around them.

Kentucky looked up at the stars as they glittered in the velvet sky.

They didn't speak for the longest time. Just two people clinging to each other in the dark, their chests rising and falling together in unison.

Part of her told her that she could still jump ship. She could make any excuse in the world to hop up and head back to the real world, where girls like her didn't get boys like him, but she wasn't going to. Kentucky had already thrown aside caution. Now she'd see what happened.

2

SHE FELT *GOOD*.

Like nothing had in a long time, Sean realized.

Wild Kentucky Lee calmed him, soothed him, made him feel as if no matter how screwed up the world was, everything would right itself.

It was so wrong.

He didn't deserve to be soothed. He didn't deserve to be reassured. Lynnie was gone and it was his fault.

He loved Lynnie. He always would. But for the last year before her death, he hadn't been *in* love with her. She was an amazing woman, to be sure. Kind, warm, intelligent and red-carpet beautiful. She belonged to another world. A world where men didn't get shredded by land mines; a world where people didn't strap bombs to children. Lynnie belonged to a world with Sunday dinners and peach cobbler. A world that didn't have a place for him.

When he ended things with her, she wasn't even

angry with him. She'd felt it, too. She just hadn't wanted to put more on his plate while he was deployed.

Then they'd had to bury her with that ring on her finger. That ring that was a symbol of how both of their dreams had died. He supposed it was fitting that it go with her.

But if he hadn't Skyped her, hadn't told her how he felt, she wouldn't have been out on that country road that night. She'd have been home, curled up in her favorite chair with her favorite tea and reading.

HE PULLED KENTUCKY CLOSER, her lush body a haven away from all that was bad. All the memories he didn't want.

This moment between them was more than just a hiding place, though. Kentucky was hot and his body responded to her as it would any sexy woman. Whereas Lynnie's appeal had been that she was so unearthly, a sort of fey loveliness with her petite pixie features and golden-blond hair, Kentucky was earthier. She was solid and strong but curved and soft. She was at odds with herself, as she was with most everything else.

Her arms were toned from her work as a mechanic, hands rough, but the swell of her hip seemed as if it'd be the most dangerous to ride. And her breasts in that lace bra… When she'd pulled off her shirt, he'd been so aroused.

Guilt had filled him, but it had done nothing to cool his desire. That was why he hadn't wanted to get in the water with her. He didn't want her to know how much of a bastard he really was.

Kentucky had always looked at him as though he were some kind of strange bug. The nicer he was to her, the odder she thought him. But underneath that, he'd always seen her secrets. When she started looking at him with a kind of longing, he knew it.

He also knew it was because he *saw* her, cared about her, and she didn't have that. She didn't have anyone she could trust. Except him. Except Lynnie.

But now Lynnie was gone.

And he wanted to lose himself in the woman next to him. For a moment, he wanted to feel something good. He wanted her to feel good, too, but he didn't want to shatter the fragile trust she'd put in him.

"Thanks for today," he said, finally breaking the silence.

"You, too." Her hand settled on his chest. "It was good to know that some things can be the same."

"But it wasn't the same."

"No? You didn't have fun? You didn't laugh? You didn't wish for a single second that we had that cordial Rachel used to swipe from her cellar and some hot dogs on that fire? Not once?"

He found himself laughing again. "Yeah, you've got me there." Sean exhaled heavily. "I've laughed more with you this evening than I in a long time."

"Well, you've got to do that for yourself now and again. Self-care, bro." She elbowed him lightly.

"Yeah, a prescription of two doses of Kentucky Lee for what ails ya?" Damn, why had he said that? Because it was exactly what he'd been thinking, and she deserved better than that. He'd punched Robbie Carter in the face for saying something similar in cruder terms when they were sophomores.

Instead of taking offense, she just laughed. Not the kind of laugh that was false, or hiding some kind pain, but a genuine belly laugh. "Sure. Why not? It's the first time I've ever been someone's cure instead of their disease."

"How do you know?"

"I don't see anyone lined up waiting for you to hand them that particular prescription."

"Once upon a time, there was a boy named Robbie Carter—"

She groaned. "Don't remind me. That's so embarrassing."

"You know?" He turned on his side to look at her.

"Wait, know what?" Her brown eyes narrowed. "Besides he didn't show to pick me up for Winter Royalty. Didn't call. Never spoke to me again."

"He thought you were the cure, so to speak."

"Funny way of showing it."

"Eric and I didn't care for the way he talked about you in the locker room."

She pushed at his shoulder. "What are you talking about?"

"He talked about how he was guaranteed to get in your pants at Royalty. He called you a slut, so I punched him."

"Once?"

"Repeatedly. Then Eric hit him. Then the rest of the team told him if he said one more word about you, they'd leave nothing left of him but a grease stain on the floor."

"Those guys never gave a damn about me. Why would they do that?"

"They cared about what Eric and I cared about. That was enough."

She sighed and flopped back on the grass. "Well, you could've told me he wasn't coming."

"We didn't want him to bail. We just wanted him to treat you with respect."

"My knights in shining armor, trying to keep me celibate since tenth grade."

"Oh, please. Don't tell me you really wanted your first time to be with Robbie Carter." They'd moved into dangerous territory, he knew. This wasn't something they should be talking about.

"Well, I did just want to get it over with. I definitely didn't want to be trite and wait until prom."

"So who was it?"

"You wouldn't know him. He lives in Canada."

"Don't go *Sixteen Candles* on me. Come on. I'll tell you mine."

"Yours was Lynnie. At Winter Royalty." She rolled her eyes, but then she smiled. "She told me all about how magical and special it was."

"Was it?" Those words punched him in the gut. "I'm glad."

"Wasn't it for you?"

"Of course it was. Then eight months later she broke up with me."

"Because she knew you were the one. She wanted to make sure neither of you ever had any regrets."

"I'll be honest—all of my junior year, I thought I was dying. I dated other girls, but there was only Lynnie." Only Lynnie, until *he* became someone else. Until his job changed him. Or maybe it unearthed who he really was, deep down in his bones. Because even though he saw horrible things, he made a difference. He loved what he did. He wished that the world didn't need people like him, but as long as it did, he'd be there in the thick of it.

"Enough about me. You already knew that. Answer my question." He searched her face. "Unless you really don't want to."

"So you're telling me the state of my virginity and nonvirginity has been a burning question plaguing you since high school?" She smirked.

"What if it has?" What was he doing? This had gone past the boundaries of their friendship. He could lie to himself and say that friends shared these details all the time, but that wasn't what this was. Not for him.

Especially because he knew not for her either.

She rolled her eyes and sighed. "Jason Carter."

"Robbie's brother?"

"I was so pissed at him that I went to his house. Jason was home from KU for winter break. He took me out to dinner and we ended up having sex in the back of his Mustang outside Paisano's."

He'd admit, he kind of hated Jason in that moment. He didn't expect to feel angry. He pushed the thoughts aside.

"Should I punch him next time I see him?" He tried to retreat, to lighten the mood.

"No, he punched himself. He married Angie Rhem."

She was super high-maintenance, and with a mean streak wider than Stranger Creek.

They laughed and then fell into that silence that seemed to keep sneaking up on them. At first it had been companionable, comfortable. Maybe even peaceful.

But now there was something between them. Something heavy and electric. Their gazes met and held, soldered together. Neither of them able or willing to break the moment.

Her lips parted, pink and soft, as she drew in tiny sharp puffs of air. The firelight cast a warm glow over them and he could see her eyes, wide dark pools he could drown in.

Sean Dryden had always believed himself to be a good guy and at this moment, if he'd been a "good guy," he'd have said something.

We shouldn't.

No, we can't.

This isn't right.

But he didn't say anything. He waited for the moment to bloom, to become whatever it was meant to be.

She reached out tentative fingers and cupped his cheek.

It was the lightest, gentlest caress, and it devastated him. In that single connection, he felt the comfort she offered him. Her grief and her understanding of his.

And of this moment. What it was. What it could be.

What it could never be.

She drew him closer and his emotions choked him. He buried his face against her breast and tightened his embrace around her, holding her so tight that nothing could ever pry her away from him.

Kentucky stroked his brow, cradled his skull and then slipped down his back only to return again.

"Share your pain with me. Let it breathe, Sean. You're not going to smother it. It'll smother you."

"How do you know?"

"I know. All the people I've lost? My parents, my aunt, Lynnie... It'll drown you. But you're not dead—they are. So don't let it." She continued her soothing caress. "I'll miss them forever. I'll love them forever. I'll even hurt because of those things, but that's not all there is to feel."

He turned his face up into her neck, his lips close to her pulse. "What if I don't deserve to feel anything else?"

"Of course you do. Lynnie loved you. She'd want to know you missed her, but she wouldn't want you to stop living because she's gone. Let yourself grieve, Sean."

"What if I'm not ready to grieve? What if I want to feel something else?" Like the softness of Kentucky's body under his while he buried himself inside her. The taste of her skin on his tongue. Her nails on his back while she screamed his name.

God, but he was a bastard.

The worst part of all this was he knew that if Lynnie could see him, she wouldn't begrudge either of them whatever solace they could find together. She'd only want them to be good to each other after.

He wasn't that noble.

"Do you want to feel, or do you want to forget?" Her touch was still soothing, but it made him burn hotter, too. "Because after the orgasm is over, you realize those things you were hiding from never left."

"Wasn't this what you wanted when you brought me out here?" He lifted his head and met her eyes. "If it's not, tell me to stop and we'll forget this ever happened."

Her eyes were luminous and open. He could see all the way to her bones. She wanted him, but she wanted more than what he was offering her.

"I don't want to forget it happened, and I especially don't want you to forget *I* happened. As good as this feels—" she shook her head "—it's not worth our friendship. I don't want to do this and then you can never look at me again because I've become a single-use item."

"I hope you'd know me better than that, Kentucky."

"Sometimes when we're hurting, we don't know ourselves."

He pushed her down in the sand and pressed her beneath him. Color was high in her cheeks and her eyes glittered in the firelight. Her arms twined around his neck. She obviously didn't give a damn that they were out in the open, that her hair was fanned out in the sand or that their wet underwear clung to them.

She was singularly focused on him.

He gripped her hips and pulled her forward to meet him, grinding his hard cock against her cleft.

"Live a little." He threw her words back at her and

his mouth descended toward hers oh-so slowly, building the heat and tension between them so they had no choice but to see where the explosion took them.

3

THIS WAS HAPPENING, Kentucky thought.

The fulfillment of a fantasy.

If she wanted it.

She could say no, deny him and herself. Or she could take her own advice and "live a little." Except she was starting to see the fallacy in that being a life philosophy. It wasn't a one-size-fits-all solution to every problem.

If she did give in to this and then he left her, it would destroy their friendship.

But her wild heart answered the question for that part of her that was afraid. If these moments between them could shatter years of friendship, then it wasn't a friendship worth having. If a simple merging of flesh was enough to lose him, she never had him to begin with.

That was the root of the problem. She wasn't ready to face that possibility. Kentucky wanted to keep the illusion a little while longer. It was a fairy tale. A night-light in an unknown darkness.

Kentucky was too old to be afraid of the dark, and too old to need stories to lull her to sleep. No, she would rather burn in the fire every time.

Even this one.

So she met his hard mouth, colliding with him in an explosion of sensation. He tasted like Scotch and mint, and the heat from his body dispelled any other further chill. She could feel nothing but him. She'd always imagined if he kissed her, it would be like this. It wouldn't be gentle touches. It would be primal, animal. Something he did by instinct, not choice.

Only he had chosen. He'd chosen to be with her here and now. He'd chosen to kiss her. He'd chosen to move his hand up her torso and beneath the damp cup of her bra.

Kentucky opened her eyes to watch him as he touched her, memorizing their joined topography, the way his tanned, callused hand looked on her breast, the shape of his thumb while he drew lazy circles around her taut pink nipple.

"Are you on any birth control? If not, I have a condom in my wallet," he said.

She shook her head. "I haven't been with anyone in a long time."

"Me neither. Not since my last deployment and I was tested when I enlisted and tested again when I was brought back Stateside. Clean bill of health. You?"

"It's been a year, but I haven't been with anyone since I was tested either."

She liked that he asked. She liked that he was mindful. Safety was incredibly sexy.

"A year? That's a long time without touch."

"But not long enough if it's not with the right some-one."

"And this, right now, is it right enough?" His eyes searched hers. He wasn't being glib; he was asking her again, giving her the chance to say no. Making sure she was going into this with both eyes open. It was such a far cry from what she'd imagined when she first began to consider that being alone with him now could lead to this.

Neither of them would be able to say this was some heated descent into madness. That it was some kind of accident where they'd been swept away by a tide of desire.

A tide of emotion maybe, but not mindless. They weren't unthinking animals, but cognizant, aware complex creatures.

"Yes, Sean."

He'd been waiting on tenterhooks, it seemed, when the expression changed on his face. He'd thought she might say no.

As if that would happen in a million years.

Still holding her gaze, he hooked his thumbs into the waist of her panties and tugged them down slowly. She bit her lip and lifted her hips to help him. His fingers sparked tiny jolts of electricity where they grazed her skin.

His lips were so close to her inner thigh, his breath ghosting against her flesh as he continued to divest her of her panties.

She tried to keep still, keep from shuddering and

quaking at every new sensation. Kentucky didn't want him to know just how bad she wanted this—him.

"Don't hide from me now. Let me see it. All of it. Show me what I do to you."

He worked his way back up her body, lips branding her as he went. First the inside of her ankle. That had never been something that struck her as particularly sexy, but the heat of his mouth on that neglected and oft-forgotten place sent shivers all through her.

Then her calf, the back of her knee—she squirmed and squealed, his breath tickling her in the most delightful way. He laughed and did it again, grasping her hips and holding her in place for the blissful torture of his mouth.

She knew exactly where he was headed with his mouth and if it could make her squeal just behind her knee, Kentucky realized she was in deep trouble.

Deep and hard trouble.

She didn't want to be anywhere else.

He moved up her thigh, tongue drawing hot little circles in her flesh.

But instead of her cleft, he continued up the softness of her belly, to the V between her breasts, to her throat—she was sure she was going to have a hickey, but she was too dizzy with lust to care.

His mouth found hers again, his hands on the back of her bra, freeing her breasts. He pulled back then and stared at her—no, *stared* was too banal a word for what he was doing. He drank her in, devoured her. She hadn't known someone's regard could become a physical thing, not like this.

She'd felt people try to stare holes in her head when they wanted to shame her into doing something or pressure her to behave differently. It felt nothing like this. The way he looked at her was intense, but it didn't try to tear her down. It made her feel like a goddess. Like something sacred and beautiful.

Something perfect.

And she needed it to stop or she'd crash down the rabbit hole. As it was, this was going to be painful when it was over. She didn't need to give that future pain any more ammunition. So she reached for his boxer briefs and pushed them down his hips.

"You're beautiful," she murmured. He was. He was perfect, as though someone had designed him for her pleasure.

"I don't have the pretty words that you deserve," he said slowly. "But you can see what you do to me." Sean drew her hand over his engorged sex.

She began to stroke him slowly and he didn't close his eyes or look away; he held her gaze. He did that a lot, looked into her eyes while doing things that would cause others to close theirs. It made it so much more intimate.

That act itself was better than any pretty words he could summon.

His flesh beneath her hand was solid, real. There was no mistaking his intent or his desire. There'd be no picking apart his words later, wondering what he really meant. Or if he was just saying flowery things to get into her pants.

This, right now, it was honest and true.

When the morning light burned this to dust, these memories would be solid and whole. She'd remember the feel of him in her palm, the way he looked into her eyes. Kentucky knew he was there with her in the moment, not taking refuge in the memory of another woman.

Even if that woman was someone they both loved.

He dipped his head and kissed her, his mouth claiming hers with renewed vigor as his hands traveled her body deliberately—bringing her pleasure was a planned military campaign.

His mouth followed the trail his hands blazed, lips hot and seeking on her heated flesh. She couldn't get enough of him. Kentucky wanted to touch him, explore him, but he was determined to indulge her first, as evidenced by the way he caught her wrists with one hand and held them over her head.

"Ladies first. I'm a gentleman." He bent between her thighs, his mouth on her mound.

She gasped and hooked her legs around his shoulders, pushing her hand through the short spikes of his hair. The scruff of a day's growth of his beard scraped against her thighs and the first touch of his tongue laving at her caused her to cry out again.

Pleasure spiraled through her and her whole body tensed with anticipation as she realized he was in no hurry. He played her body well, as if he knew exactly what she needed and set out to give it to her—as if her bliss was his own.

Kentucky was strung tight, arching her body to

meet his mouth, waiting for that burst of ecstasy and consequent unraveling of self at his hands.

He groaned as if he were savoring some particularly delicious dish and the very idea that it was her caused her channel to constrict and spasm.

Culmination struck like lightning, overtaking her when she least expected it. She'd wanted it to last longer, wanted to hold out for more. But he was giving her more, she realized, as he rose above her.

Her flesh was still quaking with aftershocks when he pushed his rigid length inside her, his face so close to hers, eyes open. They seemed to be joined intrinsically, more than skin, more than heat.

She reached up and cupped his cheek and that was when he closed his eyes. "I'm drowning in you," he murmured against her lips.

Kentucky wanted to give him that, wanted to swallow him whole and hide him from his pain so all he could feel was pleasure.

"You feel so damn good." He buried his face in her neck and she clung to him as he thrust into her.

The friction built the flame in her anew and she rolled her hips to meet his thrusts, countering his force and building their mutual gratification. His effort intensi-fied, a slow and steady increase in his speed and rhythm. Every drive forward hit the core of her, and she trembled as desire warred with fulfillment. It was as if simply by addressing her needs, he built them higher—hotter.

"Please," she begged. Kentucky didn't know what she was begging for—if she wanted to be flung off that precipice into bliss or if she wanted him to keep building their pyre higher.

His body tensed and she tightened around him, pulling him deeper as if that alone could keep him there. The tenderness was gone now as he drilled into her, and she didn't want it. She wanted this part of him, this hidden need. She gorged on it, filling herself with his pleasure, which in turn brought her own.

She shuddered with him and when he eased down next to her, she didn't let him go. Instead she pulled him closer, his head on her breast, and she stroked his cheek gently.

The moon shone down, a silent witness to what had transpired between them. Night birds sang their songs and the world around them had come alive with the darkness. This was her favorite time. Some people thought the dark to be a place of fear, but Kentucky loved how the shadows danced and saw it much like everything else—an adventure.

She wondered how long he'd stay with her like this, how long until the spell was broken. Midnight? Would he flee back to the world with his glass combat boot?

Not that it mattered so much in the grand scheme of the world. These moments were hers, for better or worse.

She shivered and it seemed to shatter the moment.

"Are you cold? We should be getting back," he said, pulling on his boxer briefs. "Wait here. I'll get your clothes."

And just like that, it was over.

He walked purposefully to the other side of the pond near Mossy Rock, where they'd disrobed. It didn't take him very long to bring her jeans and shirt back to her. There was no way she was putting a wet pair of panties and wet bra back on.

So when he handed her clothes to her, she squirmed into them commando. She wasn't sure what to say. "Thanks for the good times"? "Hey, great orgasms— I'll catch you later"?

He seemed to be at a loss, as well, looking at her, then looking away.

"Walk me back to my car?" she asked to fill the silence.

"Of course. I would never leave you out here by yourself. Remember?"

She did remember. The one time she really hadn't wanted to be around him was when she realized she had a thing for him. They'd all been hanging out, eating hot dogs they'd grilled in the fire pit, drinking a few contraband beers, and it had struck her just how perfect she thought Sean Dryden was.

That it went beyond his golden-boy image.

For the first time, she'd wished she were someone other than herself. She'd wished she were more like Lynnie so that someone like him...

She hadn't wanted to look at either of them. Felt like the biggest ass on the planet for coveting her best friend's boyfriend. She hadn't wanted to take anything away from Lynnie, but she couldn't help but wish Sean loved her instead.

She'd had trouble living in her own skin for a while

after that. Kentucky had pulled away from the group, hadn't wanted her secret desires to damage their friendships. But he wouldn't leave her alone. Lynnie seemed to understand that she needed her space, but not Sean.

"Even when I really wanted you to," she said with a half smile.

"We'll always be friends, Kentucky." His tone was low and soft, reassuring.

She didn't know if he was reassuring her or himself. "Of course we will." She stuffed her feet into her shoes.

They headed back to the path through the woods toward the seemingly distant lights of the parking lot.

With her keys in hand, she didn't look at him but instead hugged him close. "You'll be okay, soldier."

"We both will." His arms tightened around her.

As much as she wanted to linger, she knew it would only make things harder. Best to fall back into old routines so they both remembered they were still the best of friends.

"Don't leave town without saying goodbye, okay?"

"Not a chance. You, me, Rachel and Eric will grab a beer at Eddie's bar and we'll remember the good times with good friends."

She ducked away from him and slid into her car. She wouldn't have looked at him if he hadn't put his hand on her shoulder and demanded she stop.

"Take care of yourself, Kentucky."

"If I don't, no one else will." She flashed him a lop-sided grin and drove away, secure in the knowledge that the night at Eddie's wasn't going to happen and she'd probably never see him again.

Her heart ached, but it wasn't empty. It was full of tonight. Of memories.

Of what was and what could've been.

For all of them.

4

KENTUCKY WAS WORKING on restoring a cherry-red '57 Chevy. It was a beautifully old dame who still sparked with a fire that Kentucky needed in her life. She'd done the interior in this white metallic-flake vinyl and was currently installing various chrome accessories.

Working on that car was like meditating for her. Nothing could intrude on her thoughts while she was working on Betty, as she'd named the lovely machine. She could lose herself in the intricacies of the old girl's guts, in the repetition of shining the chrome. Betty was close to done, though, and Kentucky would need a new project soon.

If she kept avoiding thinking about Sean, as she'd done since last night, she'd be able to restore a whole fleet of the '57s.

When her cell rang from the pocket of her coveralls, she jerked it out, hoping against hope it would be Sean—even though the logical part of her brain knew it wasn't.

It was Rachel. "Hey, Pop-Tart. Are you banging away on Betty?" she teased.

"You know it." She was always working on Betty in every second of free time she had. Originally, Kentucky began restoring her in hopes of selling her at a profit, but the car had come to mean so much more to her. Betty had come to represent a dream of something more. A dream where Kentucky could cruise off down the highway and end up in a place that was her idea of heaven. Just as soon as Betty was done, they'd be on the road.

She knew it was silly, that every place and every person had their own faults, their own quirks, but Kentucky needed something to believe in and Betty had become that for her.

"Yeah, well, go wash off the grease and put on your good boots. Guess who is in town?"

"I don't know. Tell me."

"It's no fun if you don't guess."

Had Sean called her about going to Eddie's? She wasn't ready for anyone to know what happened between them last night, and she was sure that Sean wasn't really looking to circulate that information either. She swallowed and her gut flipped over and tied itself in knots. "I guess I'm not that much fun these days."

"Sean! He just called and asked if I could get us together for some beers and pool tonight at Eddie's."

Suddenly, the idea of seeing him again, pretending as though she didn't have deeper feelings for him after what they'd done—it was like a knife in her chest. So much for not letting anything come between them. So much for her acting as if it were just sex and didn't matter past the comfort they'd managed to give each other in the moment.

She kind of despised herself for having all of the feelings she promised herself she wouldn't.

"Man, I don't know. I'm almost done with Betty. I could probably finish her tonight if I don't go."

"Come out and celebrate. Come on, how often is Sean home? It'll be fun." Rachel sighed heavily. "I think he really needs this, Kentucky. He didn't sound good when I spoke to him. Didn't sound like himself."

"Well, his fiancée died less than a year ago," she offered hesitantly.

"All the more reason for us to be together."

"What time are you meeting?"

"Seven."

She was torn between wanting to go and wanting to get rid of the resurgence of her feelings for him. If they saw each other and he acted as if everything were cool, she could make it that way in her head. She wasn't stupid. She knew she was no Lynnie.

And she didn't want to be. She'd wished it when she was young, that she could be someone else. But she was right with who she was now. She wasn't changing for anyone. Even golden-boy Sean Dryden.

There was only one Lynnie, and she was gone and wasn't ever coming back.

"What's with all this reluctance to hang out with Sean? Don't you want to see him?"

Rachel was much too close to her secret. "Just have things to do, is all. I'll be there. Save me a seat."

Her stomach flipped again, and so did her heart,

the traitorous bastard. If Sean really wanted to see her again as something outside their friendship, he'd have called himself. This was a message and she'd received it loud and clear.

But she'd go.

Hell, maybe she should go crazy and curl her hair.

That was just what she did. Kentucky even put on a red lip gloss that tasted just like cherries. She had to admit that she cleaned up nice. She liked the woman in the mirror looking back at her and maybe even thought she was just a little bit pretty.

When she walked into Eddie's a short time later, Rachel and Eric were already there.

"Whoa, nice!" Eric grinned. "Is that for me?"

"Nah, you know I'm trying to steal your girl." Kentucky grinned back.

Rachel laughed and tugged Kentucky down into her lap. "You can steal me anytime, sugar."

She found herself lost in the moment, and just like old times, she reached over and swiped a sip of Rachel's beer.

"So who is up for a game?" Eric nodded to the pool tables.

"I'll totally kick your ass, soldier," Rachel promised.

"Not with a lap of Kentucky, you won't."

"Bet me." Rachel lifted her chin.

"Shall we say a kiss?"

"Gross," Kentucky interjected. "Let me just get out of the way here." She squirmed off Rachel's lap.

She was so happy that Eric and Rachel had found each other. Rachel had had a thing for Eric since they were kids. Her emotions had always been kind of tattooed on her face for everyone to see, but Eric… Eric was more like a rock when it came to his emotions.

"You wouldn't think it was gross if you had your own soldier. I know this guy…" Eric started.

Kentucky held up her hand. "Lord save me from well-intentioned big-brother types. Sean told me what you guys did."

Eric wore an expression of practiced innocence, eyes wide. "Who? Me?"

"Yeah, that doesn't work on anyone who knows you, brother." She elbowed him lightly.

"Especially not me," Sean said, surprising them.

Rachel was the first to throw her arms around him and hug him as if it were going out of style. Sean returned the embrace, rubbing his hand up and down her back.

Eric didn't bother to hide his emotion at seeing the other man. He clapped his hands on his back and hugged him tight. They stayed that way longer than what was considered appropriate for a casual hug, although it was anything but casual. Sean was his brother in all ways but biological.

"It's good to see you," Eric said gruffly.

"It's been too long. Sorry about that, man." Sean returned the hug with just as much ferocity.

There was enough emotion hanging among the group of them that it was almost a physical presence.

When Eric stepped away from Sean, his arms were open again. This time for Kentucky.

That emotion that hung heavy before, this time it was like a wall and it kept her from leaping into his arms the way she wished she could. The way she would've before Mossy Rock.

"What, no love for me, my pretty Kentucky Lee?" Sean looked so earnest, so hopeful and so...

Her throat constricted. "Always." She leaned into his embrace, carefully. Almost as if all her feelings were something dirty and she was afraid to sully his crisp white T-shirt with them.

He smelled so good, felt so good...like all things pure and true.

The embodiment of the dream she couldn't have.

Sean rubbed up and down her back just as he had with Rachel, but he tightened the embrace, crushing her against his chest in a way that made her wish they were alone and she could tear that shirt off him and drown in the heat of him, in the sensation of their bodies together.

"You smell good, pretty girl."

Her face flushed at the compliment and he let her go.

"So we playing some pool or what?"

"You and Sean first." Rachel nodded to the guys. "I need Kentucky for some girl time." She didn't wait for a response but practically dragged Kentucky to the bathroom.

As soon as the door closed behind them, Rachel turned to face her and leaned her back against the door. "Okay, what the hell was that?"

"I don't have any idea what you're talking about." Kentucky forced her expression to remain neutral. Why had she thought she could keep any of this a secret from Rachel? Rachel had gone into hyper matchmaker mode since she'd started dating Eric. She said she wanted everyone to be as happy as she was, whether they wanted to be or not.

Rachel put her hand on her hip. "Really? That's the answer we're going with?"

"Yep."

"You saw Sean last night, didn't you? What happened?"

"I—" She didn't want to lie to Rachel, but she wasn't about to go spreading tales that weren't only hers to tell. "It's not something I can or want to talk about. Just let it go, okay?"

"Uh, no." Rachel sighed. "Fine. But you know whatever happened, you can talk to me."

Kentucky considered the distance between them, the hole that had been left in their friendship, their world, since Lynnie died. "Yeah, I know. But you know I'm not the confiding kind. This girl thing, the talking in the bathroom at the pool hall, that's not me."

Rachel smiled, her features soft, with understanding in her eyes. "No, but you can be if you need to be. We're all still walking wounded after losing her."

"I know that, too. Don't say anything to Eric, okay?"

"I won't have to. He saw the way you and Sean were together, but I'll tell him to keep his opinion to himself."

"Would he be angry?"

"What, if you and Sean were a thing?" Rachel turned her head to the side.

Kentucky chewed her lip. "Yeah, I mean, he's Lynnie's brother."

"I really think he'd just want you both to be happy." She sighed. "I don't know if I should tell you this."

"Then don't. Whatever it is, I'll wait for Sean to tell me if he wants to."

"When did you get to be the mature one in the group?" Rachel hugged her again.

All of this hugging was not something she was usually into, but lately, it had been kind of nice. "I don't know. But I think we need to fix that because it's definitely a sign of the impending apocalypse."

"You know how much Lynnie loved you, right?"

"Yeah." She nodded. "And we have each other to remind ourselves of her. I think she's still with us. In you. In me. In Eric." Kentucky swallowed hard. "In Sean."

Rachel nodded. "So whatever happens, don't let it make things weird."

"I won't." Or she'd try like hell. But change was inevitable. It happened to everything. Especially people, friendships—that was just the way of life.

"So, even with my eyes watering from all the feels, how do I look?" Rachel tucked her hair behind her ear.

"Like you got up on Eric's side of the bed," she teased.

Rachel slapped her arm and blushed. "Well, you know…"

Kentucky held up her hand. "This is all the girl talk I can handle at the moment. This is my quota for the night." But she softened her words with a grin. "So next time give me the juicy details first and then we won't have time to talk about me."

They made their way back to the table, next to which Eric and Sean had already started a game of pool. Kentucky grabbed her own beer and sat down to watch. Rachel didn't hesitate to harass Eric while he was trying to make a shot, blowing in his ear, tickling his neck, rubbing up against his back.

Sean shot her a look that seemed to be one of sympathy for Eric. Kentucky shrugged as if to say, "What can you do?"

Suddenly, she found a pool stick shoved in her face.

"Take over my light work, huh, Kentucky?" Eric asked. "I'm obviously not getting anywhere, since Rachel wants to dance."

She accepted the stick and approached the table, trying to figure out a strategy to beat Sean.

"We could start over," Sean offered.

"Nah, I like a challenge." She continued to study the table.

He moved silently, stealthily, and slid up beside her, his arm around her waist. "You sure you don't want to start over?"

She had the idea he was talking about something other than the game, but she didn't quite understand what he meant.

God, but he smelled good. Playing any game with him in proximity was definitely going to be a challenge. She couldn't concentrate. All she could think about was him bending her over the pool table, pulling her hair and taking her right there.

"I don't need to start over. I can play the hand that's dealt me. Or in this case, the balls." Jeez, that sounded way dirtier than what she meant.

"Oh, really?" He arched his brow and flashed her a smirk.

She felt her face go hot again and knew she had to be blushing, but she wasn't embarrassed. Or at least, that was what she told herself, and she certainly wasn't going to let Golden Boy outdo her.

On anything.

"Yeah, really." She slid her fingers up and down the end of the pool cue slowly and with obvious purpose. "I'm extra good with this, too." Kentucky leaned over the table. "Nine and eleven in the corner pocket."

She took her shot and the balls followed her prediction and dipped into the pocket. Kentucky took her next shot but succeeded only in setting up the next play.

"I guess you handle your balls well."

She leaned over the table again, examining all possible outcomes to the game, plotting her strategy, and tried not to think about the innuendo. Before Mossy Rock, she'd have played this game until they both ran out of puns and the double entendres were so ridiculous they both laughed until their stomachs hurt.

But now she thought about him touching her. Thought about how she wanted to do all those things with him again.

He took his shot and completely missed.

"You're cheating," he accused, but his tone was light. Teasing.

"What do you mean?"

"Don't act like you didn't do that on purpose. You're much craftier than that."

She looked down at where he pointed and saw that the V-neck of her shirt gave him a rather spectacular view of her pink lacy bra and the curves of the tops of her breasts.

Kentucky kept trying to ignore the butterflies in her belly, the burn between her legs as she thought of him looking at her body and being so entranced that he missed his shot. "You're right, I am much craftier than that." She swallowed her fear and decided to let the conversation take them where it would instead of trying so hard to monitor her feelings, her thoughts and what she had to say about them.

"If I was going to do that on purpose, I'd give you a flash and then tell you that I'm wearing a lacy thong that matches."

Sean's grin faltered and was replaced with something hot and intense. Something that made his eyes burn right through her.

"Then I'd tell you I'm not wearing it. Or any other underwear. And I'd bend over the table and show you. But I think that would be something to save for a tie-breaker match. What do you think?"

Had she really just said that? So much for pretending that last night hadn't happened.

She'd never have said anything with any serious intent to him before. Innuendo, sure. But this went so far beyond that.

His knee slid between hers and his grip squeezed her waist. "You're playing with fire."

Her heart slammed against her chest. "Am I? Do you think I'll get burned?"

"You might."

"I'm a big girl and I do like my matches." It was

true—she was a "leap first, think later" kind of girl. "Especially when the fire burns so hot."

"But burn it does, and it reduces all the kindling to ash and memory."

"I still love the blaze."

"I suppose you would. Some of us aren't used to the smell of kerosene."

His knee crept higher, the friction of the denim with his heat causing frissons of awareness to thrill through her.

He knew what he was doing. He was the one who'd said this was a one-time thing. Now it felt as if he was taunting her.

She broke the connection. "Then maybe you should go take a cold shower."

5

SHE WAS RIGHT. Sean should go take a cold shower, but he knew from experience that would do little to extinguish his lust.

After the lake, he'd gone back to the sparse extended-stay room he'd rented and showered in ice-cold water in the hopes it would wash away the pond, his guilt and his desire for Kentucky.

No such luck. Even after their encounter, he'd been hard and ready for her again. Sean wanted to lose himself in her over and over again. He wanted to drown in her hair, in the scent of her, the feel of her, in the softness of her body. How perfect the world was when he was buried between her thighs.

He'd acted as though it couldn't happen again, as though he didn't want it to happen again. But he did. He wanted it too much.

He wanted her too much.

Sean knew he'd made her into a kind of savior, an ideal on a pedestal. Which was strange in itself because he'd never known a woman less fey than Kentucky Lee. She was earthy, real. No marionette of spun glass and spiderwebs, but real. Whole.

Maybe she'd become his ideal somewhere along the way because she wasn't the type of woman who broke. Or at least, that was what she showed the world.

Sean knew without a doubt this thing between them would break her.

He knew that she had feelings for him, always had. Knew that she was in love with him.

He loved her, but he wasn't in love with her. Never would be. He didn't know if he could be in love. Sean loved his job, but it required a certain disconnect to do what he did. A certain level of surrender and nonattachment.

It wasn't fair to do this to her.

But Jesus Christ, when she said things like that, about not wearing any panties and showing him, he wanted to see it. He wanted to call her to the mat, then mount her on it.

Just as he would on this damn pool table.

Devil help them all if she actually had leaned over the pool table and shown him her bare cleft, all moist and slick for him, splayed for his view.

His cock was so rigid he probably didn't need the cue to shoot.

Instead of releasing her, he only stepped closer. "You're not wrong, Kentucky. I should go take a shower. I should submerge myself in ice, but it wouldn't do any good. Not with your perfect ass in that skirt and your dirty little mouth telling me everything that's not under it. That you're bare."

"Maybe I was just talking shit. Maybe there's a thong under there. Maybe there are high-waisted granny panties." She leaned back against him just a little bit, but in that action was submission.

Surrender to what he wanted from her.

He hadn't thought he could get any harder.

"Maybe, but now you're wondering what it would be like if I bent you over this pool table and I'm wondering what your hair looks like splayed on that green felt."

She shivered delicately. "So what if I am? I wonder a lot of things."

"Hey, Kentucky. If you'd told me you needed instruction on how to hold the cue, I'd have been happy to help," a guy from across the bar said.

Sean had fantasies of punching him in the face for speaking to her that way but realized that he'd spoken to her the same way. Treated her like a disposable thing just because he wanted her. Wanted the solace she offered and, more than that, the pleasure.

"Yeah, you're good at holding the cue. You do it every night by yourself," Kentucky tossed back.

"You're a mean woman, Kentucky Lee."

"And don't forget it, Billy Doniphan."

The guy held up his beer like a salute to Sean and nodded.

"It's like he wants to die," Sean grumbled.

Kentucky laughed, the sound melodic. "Oh, please. You don't need to get into any fights over my honor. I've been turning him down since high school. He thinks you're some kind of superman for getting this close to me."

"He doesn't respect you."

"Do you?" She turned and faced him, placing her palms on his shoulders.

Her touch was like a brand. "Of course I do." Sean leaned closer to her, brought her against him and danced with her to whatever sad, slow ballad was howling from the jukebox—the game of pool forgotten.

"That's why I'm having such a hard time with last night."

"I thought we weren't going to let it change us," she whispered.

"Me, too, but it did. Because I can't stop thinking about touching you."

"Then maybe you should touch me while you can."

"Then what, Kentucky?"

"I don't know." She swayed against him in time to the music. "But if we've already changed, we can't pretend like we haven't."

"Why not?"

"Because it hurts and right now nothing has to hurt." She moved her palms from his shoulders to his back and pressed herself even more intimately against him. "It can just be about what feels good."

"And then when I leave?"

"Then you leave. I know you're not looking for love. You're looking for comfort, solace, a surcease of sorrow."

"And I'm looking to use you to do that. To fill myself up with all you want to give me until it doesn't hurt anymore. Until the night isn't so dark. But I have nothing to give you in return."

"Did I ask you for anything?" She looked up at him, eyes wide and luminous in the half-light. "And before you tell me I don't know what to ask for, believe me... I do. I also know that I'm a grown woman who doesn't need you or Eric telling me what I deserve or what I want." She leaned into him again, brushing her cheek against him, her breath a soft tease on his neck.

"Maybe I want something to lose myself in, too. Maybe I'm feeling how alone I am with a singular intensity and maybe I want to put a Band-Aid on it. Maybe I want to use you to do it."

She described exactly what he was feeling, what he was afraid of.

"But you know what we do with Band-Aids, right? We throw them away." Something dark twisted in his gut.

"Neither one of us are Band-Aids. We're people. I'm not going to throw you away after you make the pain stop. You told me last night if I thought that about you, that I didn't know you very well. What's changed?"

"I guess what's changed is that I see what you want from me, Kentucky. I see you. I've always seen you." She stilled in his arms, stood motionless. "But I want something from you, too, and it's only a pale imitation of what you deserve. You shouldn't accept anything but everything, if you know what I'm saying."

"Here I thought I kept my secrets well hidden." She didn't try to deny it. He loved that about her—she was so honest, so raw. He couldn't imagine living that way, with his insides exposed to the world in that unapologetic manner.

"Not from me. Lynnie never saw that want in you. You did hide it well from everyone but me. I know you like I know myself."

"Then you should also know that I wouldn't offer you what I can't handle."

"Yes, you would. You'd give me the world because that's who you are."

"Don't let that get out," she half laughed, and pulled away from him to look up at him. "You've made me into some kind of martyr, and, Sean, I'm anything but. If I were a martyr, I'd have never taken you to Mossy Rock. I wouldn't be here with you now hoping that your hands don't stay on my waist. Or wondering if the stockroom in the back has a lock on the door."

"It does." He knew he shouldn't have gone there, shouldn't have focused on the part of that statement where he got exactly what he wanted. He wasn't protecting her; he wasn't being a good friend. He was being the worst kind of bastard, preying on her wants and needs to get what he wanted when he knew in the end it would hurt her.

She took his hand silently and guided him back to the storeroom and he followed her obediently as if he were the one being led down the path to his own demise.

Kentucky locked the door behind him.

He searched her eyes for a long moment looking for regret, for desire, for his own absolution.

The only thing he saw there was her offering him everything he wanted on a platter.

So he took it.

His lips crashed into hers, rough and demanding. Instead of meeting him head-to-head, she melted beneath him, became pliable in his arms with her mouth opening under his like the unfurling of tender rosebuds in a thunderstorm.

He could've laughed at his own description. Sean Dryden didn't talk that way, didn't think that way, but something about Kentucky made him want to find the pretty words. Made him dig through the darkness for the light, made him want to lay those pretty things at her feet.

Sean remembered what she'd said about touching her until he could stop thinking about her, basically until he stopped wanting her. He wondered if that would ever happen. It was almost as if her body were a drug and now that he'd had his first hit, he couldn't stop.

Didn't want to stop.

She felt better than anything had in so long.

Better than the last time he'd been with Lynnie.

He'd been so afraid of soiling her, of breaking her, of tarnishing her with all of the dark things he had to see and do. He'd just wanted to protect her.

With Kentucky, the only pain he could cause her wasn't the kind he could protect her from. Even if he walked away from her now, he'd already crossed that line.

They'd *both* already crossed the line.

He slid his hand up between her legs, satisfying his curiosity as to what was beneath that tight little skirt.

His fingers came into contact with soft silk—so not bare, and not a lacy thong at all.

Demure but sexy little silk panties. He wanted—no, needed—to know if they were pink just like her bra. Pink like the inside of her pretty pussy. Sean stroked his finger back and forth over the material until it was damp and she was breathless.

He lifted her and sat her on top of the metal storage rack whose shelves were full of bottles of hard cider and imported beer. She leaned back and anchored herself, gripping the edges of the sturdy shelf.

Sean pulled her panties down her long legs and stuffed them in his pocket. He angled her legs open and pressed his mouth to the inside of her knee. It was tender and sensitive. She shivered with each caress as he moved up her thigh, his fingers holding her knees wide.

He wanted to taste her again, her essence on his tongue. He wanted to drive her wild so she was as addicted to him as he was to her.

He loved the taste of her, the way she squirmed to get closer to him, the way her thighs tensed when she was close to her orgasm.

He licked and laved, his cock swollen and thick, seemingly more so with every caress, every slide of his tongue over her engorged pink flesh.

This angle was amazing. He was going to have to invest in metal shelves everywhere he ever lived. It gave him an unfettered view and easy access.

Sean grabbed her ass and pulled her forward toward his mouth. He did all the things to her with his tongue he wanted to do with other parts of his body—thrusting his tongue inside her the same as he would his cock or his fingers.

She loved every second of it, her smothered, breathy cries fueling him onward.

"Please," she begged.

"Please more? Yeah," he said, ghosting his breath over her slit.

He continued the campaign until she was shuddering against him and he could taste the evidence of her pleasure on his lips.

Sean was good at this, at reading her body and giving her exactly what she needed. He took pride in that and loved the little sounds she made as she surrendered to ecstasy.

He dropped his jeans, cock hard and at the ready. Sean used the condom he'd pulled from his wallet and worked it down his erection before lifting her easily from the metal shelves and sliding her down his body until he'd impaled her on his cock.

For Sean, it was like the dawn. The feeling of her around him, pulling him deeper, banished all the darkness in his head. The loneliness, the fear and, for a moment, even the guilt.

She clung to him, her forehead resting against his, her breath sweet on his lips. He wanted to taste her mouth, wanted her to taste her own pleasure on their lips.

Kentucky gasped when their lips met and he lost himself in her, let himself drown in her pleasure.

He pressed her against the wall, hips thrusting up to bury himself deep inside her and she leaned her head back, seeming to be completely oblivious to everything but him. She obviously trusted him to hold her up, to take her higher, to make her come again.

Her interior walls tensed around him again as her pleasure reached its pinnacle and he spilled inside her.

Even with his knees weak and his body still frenetic from his release, he didn't want to put her down.

When he put her down, when they broke apart, he'd have to face the world again. The pain. The shame.

He'd have to examine what he'd done.

What he'd do again if she let him.

It was as if she knew. "Stay here with me a moment longer," she said.

So Sean did, because he didn't want the intrusion of the outside world any more than she did.

Would Eric and Rachel know what had happened?

Not that he cared, not really. Eric would warn him off, but not because of Lynnie. He'd confided in Eric about his feelings, or lack of feelings, for Lynnie before he'd spoken to her about it. No, Eric would want him to consider Kentucky, to consider what the consequences of their choices were more than what was a healing balm in the moment.

He'd be right.

But neither of them could seem to stop.

She wrapped her arms around him tight, clung to him, and he held her there. As if that could hold the moment with them.

"The way this feels right now, I wish we could stay here." Her voice was quiet and low.

"Me, too. But the world didn't stop spinning. We should get back out there."

"Okay. You go first. I'll follow."

He kissed her again, tasting their passion on her mouth. "Kentucky—" he began.

"No, we're not doing regrets."

"I have to see you again," he blurted.

"Okay. You can come to the garage tomorrow. I live upstairs."

"Are you sure?" he asked. "I'm still not offering anything."

"I'm still not asking." She shoved him toward the door. "This can be good. At least until you leave. Don't screw it up by overanalyzing it."

He knew better.

He knew better than to believe that this would do anything but crash and burn. He knew better than to take what was happening between them at face value, especially when he knew what was on the other side of the coin. He knew better than to think this wasn't going to end them.

But he would follow her down that primrose path to hell anyway.

6

"So, you and Dryden a thing?" Billy asked when he found her outside Eddie's.

Sean was still inside talking with Rachel and Eric, but she needed some room to breathe. Space to think. Perhaps talk some sense into herself.

She inhaled the warm summer air and looked up at the sky. It was different now; the stars were different. The way they hung, burning and oblivious to the travails of the tiny creatures below. The sky wasn't different, she supposed. She was.

This was the same sky she'd looked up at the night before she'd been with Sean. The same sky after.

But everything was different.

"No," she finally answered him.

"You're not the type to go into storerooms with guys on a whim," he said.

"How would you know? Just because I've never been in a storeroom with you?" she tossed back, defensive. She didn't want to be prey for the rumor mill. Especially not for all the women who'd been practically foaming at the mouth at Lynnie's funeral to get a piece of Sean.

She turned to look at Billy. "We just had some things to talk through. That's all."

"There wasn't any talking. Some moaning, maybe. But no talking."

"I have no idea what you're talking about." She pursed her lips and met his eyes evenly, trying to stare him down. Some part of her hoped if she stared long enough, her ire would melt that memory from his brain and they'd never need speak of it again.

"I guess it's none of my business."

"Nope," she agreed easily.

"But you know, there are more guys walking the earth than Sean Dryden."

"What do you mean?"

"Me, that's what I mean."

"Yeah, I know you're a guy." She teased him because she didn't want to have this discussion. Billy was a sweet country boy who'd been her friend for a long time. But she never had any interest in him.

It made her think of her situation with Sean. She tried to imagine a scenario where she turned to Billy for comfort the way Sean had turned to her. The idea of his hands on her, while it wasn't repulsive, did nothing for her at all.

She wondered if that was the way Sean thought about her.

No, no. It couldn't be. Not after what had just happened in the storeroom. She'd just told him not to over-analyze it, so she wasn't going to do that either. She wasn't going to pick apart each interaction and try to make it more or less than it was.

"Kentucky, you know what I mean. No man has ever been able to make any headway with you since you first laid eyes on Dryden. His halo is blinding you to everything else."

"You can't help who you love."

"I guess that's true." Billy nudged her. "Because, girl, even though I wish I didn't feel this way, you're it for me."

"I was trying to save you the confession."

"Words like that aren't meant to be saved. To be hidden. You got to speak them to the world and let them breathe."

"Well, that's nothing short of terrifying." She laughed, unsure of what else to say to him. How to comfort him without hurting him.

"Not so much. I lose nothing by telling you I care about you. A wild thing like you should know that."

But she could lose everything—especially the fantasy that someday Sean Dryden would be in love with her. She liked having someday. She liked being able to hold that close and hope.

Sean knew how she felt. She wasn't going to tell him, beat that dead horse into the ground. Neither was she going to deny herself these days with him. She could practice recrimination and regret after he was gone, although she'd never been a big fan of either.

"Billy, you're a sweet guy."

"Oh, hell, we don't need to go there. I don't need the nice-guy talk." Billy grinned. "I just wanted you to know when whatever's going on with you is done, I'll be here." He patted her back in an oddly platonic gesture and went back inside.

"What are you doing out here?" Rachel asked her as she pushed her way past Billy.

"Man, y'all keep filling up my dance card. I just wanted some quiet. Too many people inside, too much noise. You know me. I'm kind of a loner sometimes."

"Sean is inside getting hammered. What did you say to him?"

"Nothing." She brushed her hands on her skirt. "Look, I'm going to go. I'm tired."

"Are you sure? I can have Eric drive you home."

"No, no. Stay. I'm good. I'll call you later." She shoved her hands in her pockets. "I know I don't have to tell you, but…"

"I'll make sure Sean gets home okay."

Kentucky gave her a half smile. "Good."

He wasn't doing well, but he'd made it clear what he wanted from her. It wasn't her friendship or a shoulder to lean on. It was sex.

So she'd done what she could for the night.

She started walking back to the garage and she'd made it about a block when the sound of a truck's engine caused her to turn and look.

Billy rolled down the window. "You want a ride?"

"No, I'm good."

"Are you sure? Let me drop you at the garage."

"Okay." She climbed up into his truck and they drove the short distance to her garage in silence.

"Thanks for the ride," she said when they pulled up to the parking lot.

"You can make it up to me."

"Oh, can I?" She waited for him to say something that would make her regret thinking he was such a nice guy.

"Yeah. Get me in for transmission service on this next week." He patted the door of the truck.

"Sure thing. Bring it by and I'll get it done." She went inside and locked the door, watching through the window to see that Billy was on his way before turning out the light.

She wandered over to Betty, the sleek red '57, and leaned against the familiar metal of the door, running her fingers over the exterior. Yeah, she was still the embodiment of a dream. Of freedom.

Of hope.

But in a different way. She didn't need to escape herself anymore. For a long time, she hadn't realized that was what cars meant to her—a way to hide from everything she didn't have and all the things she thought she wasn't supposed to want.

"Why'd you leave with him?" A voice from the other side of the car scared the crap out of her.

"God Almighty, Sean. What the hell are you doing?"

"I need to know."

"So you broke into my garage? How did you even get here before me?"

"I ran."

"But you've been drinking like a fish."

"I've been drinking. Trying to keep numbing my guilt, but I'm not numb. I'm not drunk."

"So you broke into my garage and scared ten years

off my life?" She studied him. "Because why? I got a ride home from Billy Doniphan?"

"You sure as hell didn't leave with me. So yeah, why him?"

"Because he offered me a ride." She put her hands on her hips. "What's with the inquisition here?"

"I looked up and you were just gone, Kentucky."

He sounded so wounded. "What do you want from me?"

"I thought I knew."

"Do you want to crash on my couch tonight?" She wanted to offer him the bed with her, but that was too much like the relationship he said he didn't want.

Hell, maybe she didn't want it either.

The Sean Dryden she'd fallen for would never have shown up at her house blitzed or broken into her garage. This, more than anything else, showcased that he wasn't the same guy who'd left Winchester.

She couldn't let herself forget that he'd been to war. He was a spec ops pilot with all the duties, honor and horror that entailed. He wasn't the golden boy anymore. He was a man who'd been through hell.

"I want to sleep with you. When I touch you, nothing hurts. So maybe if I sleep next to you, nothing will hurt in my dreams either. I won't see her. She won't tell me over and over again how her death was my fault."

She hadn't thought her heart could break for him any more, but just then she realized how wrong she'd been.

"Lynnie would never say that to you, Sean. Never."

"I know that. But it doesn't stop me from hearing her voice in my dreams."

"I don't think anyone can help you with that but you." She reached out a hand to touch his face.

"I'll go."

"No." She took his hand. "Stay."

He pulled her against him carefully and rested his chin on her head, as if comforting her. Only she knew it was he who needed the comfort. She took his hand and led him up into her apartment toward the bedroom.

This was intimacy. This was the part of a relationship he didn't want. It wasn't just being beholden to another person; it was sharing this deeper part of himself.

She didn't need him to tell her that to know.

Kentucky left the lights off, almost as if that would keep all the things she was feeling in the dark, too.

He sat down on the side of the bed, facing away from her, and took off his shoes and his shirt.

She stripped down to only her panties and slid between the sheets.

He stayed seated for a long time before he joined her, but he still had his back to her.

"It's my fault, you know."

"Lynnie?" she whispered.

"Yeah."

"How?" She wasn't going to shoot him some reassurance just to placate him. He'd come to confess and she'd let him.

"The night she died, I called her." He took a deep, shuddering breath. "I broke it off."

Conflicting emotions warred within her. "Why in the world would you ever break it off with someone like her?"

"My love for her changed. I changed. *We* changed." He was silent again for a long moment. "I guess we could've still found some measure of happiness. But our worlds were too different. She was the cheerleader turned kindergarten teacher. That life would've been a lie for me. I've got blood on my hands, and it wouldn't be so bad if I felt guilty for it. But I don't. That's a part of me I could never let her see. A part of me that isn't going to change."

"She'd have loved you even if she saw it."

"I know." His voice was low, harsh. "It would've broken something in her, though. You know that, too."

Kentucky tried not to think about gentle Lynnie trying to process the horrors of war. Of the man Sean had become. Reconciling the good man he was with the horrible things he'd had to do. He was right.

"I'm sorry."

"So was I. So was she. We're all sorry." He sighed. "But you understand now, right? If I hadn't called her and told her, she wouldn't have been out on that road. You know how Lynnie loved to drive whenever she had something she needed to work out."

"It wasn't your fault, Sean. I'm not going to beat you over the head with it, because it won't matter until you decide it for yourself. But you have no control over what Lynnie chose to do or not do. She was her own person. Just like you."

He didn't answer her.

"She wouldn't blame you. You know that."

"I do, which is why I have to do it for her. She was always too forgiving for her own good."

"Does Eric know?"

"I talked to him before I made the call."

"And what does he say?"

"The same thing you do."

Kentucky scooted closer to him and put her arm around his waist and rested her cheek against his back.

"I tried so hard to save her, Kentucky. But I broke her anyway."

"You didn't break her. You don't give her enough credit." She stroked her fingers down over his biceps. "Lynnie was a lot of things. She was sweet, she was kind, but she was never weak. She'd never let you break her."

"You didn't see the same side of her I did."

"I could say the same to you."

"She was so soft, so fragile, Kentucky." He rolled over to face her. "But you're not. You're not soft at all."

His hands moved down her hips, to between her thighs.

"Except here. Here—" he slipped his fingers beneath the silk of her panties and thrust up into her "—you're soft and sweet, but you're made to be filled with everything I can give you."

His words were a kind of trespass; he was hiding in their lust from his pain. She wanted to tell him no. That was a lie. She wanted to be strong enough to tell him no. Kentucky wanted to make him face his pain.

She wanted him to see her as more than a temporary fix.

He said he wouldn't treat her that way, but he already was. He was feeling so many emotions he didn't want to feel, and instead of processing them, he'd made the situation sexual. In a strange way, he'd taken away the intimacy because this was on defined, temporary terms.

And she'd agreed to it.

He was basically telling her that he didn't worry about breaking her, and on one hand, she loved that. On the other, she wondered if it was because he cared if he broke Lynnie but not her.

She shook the thought from her head. She wasn't going to do this to herself. She knew what she'd signed up for with him and it was what she wanted.

Would she really want a relationship with him? Maybe the guy he was before, the high school football all-star who was a sweet kid with an earnest smile. But the man he was now? He wasn't sweet, and while he was still earnest, he didn't have that small-town innocence anymore.

He'd seen the darker things in the world and he'd chosen them.

And she, she was choosing him; she was choosing this moment. She was choosing to feel everything, to let it all burst within her no matter which road her feelings took. She grabbed his shoulders and shifted so that he rolled atop her. "So fill me."

He did.

Almost as if they were in a dream, he slid her panties down her legs, never breaking eye contact. He pinned her there with his gaze, the intensity making her helpless and unwilling to move for fear of breaking this cobra-like spell. She'd never been big on being prey, until now.

Kentucky was held in complete thrall and she loved every second of it.

He hadn't put on a condom this time, and she didn't want him to. She wanted this connection with him. She could get the morning-after pill from the pharmacy tomorrow.

Because the intimacy between them was still there.

It made every touch more intense, every sigh more meaningful and every jolt of pleasure more electric.

He was inside her, skin to skin; they were irrevocably linked.

This was what she'd wanted from him, something real. Something that she could remember in the light of day and never doubt that it had happened.

Maybe this was just a moment, but it was their moment. It was something no one could take away from them. No one could change it.

She wrapped her legs around his hips, but she didn't pull him down closer. Kentucky wanted to watch his face. She wanted to see what she did to him, the passion they wove together.

Each thrust was a deliberate, concise action. There was no wild frenetic energy here. It was all a controlled burn, the blaze between them set with purpose and manipulated to burn hotter with a single intent: their mutual release.

Kentucky was on the edge, but she didn't want to fall alone. Her orgasm hit her hard and fast, unexpected.

"You're so wild, Kentucky. Watching you come is like being wrapped in a storm."

She gasped in his ear, "And you said you didn't have pretty words."

He continued to push into her, surrendering to his own culmination.

Sean eased off her body and onto his back next to her in the bed. He pulled her against him, smoothing her hair away from her face.

"This is only going to end badly, Kentucky. We both know it, but neither of us can stop it."

"Like I said, Sean, let's just let it be what it is. This feels too good to deny ourselves, and it doesn't hurt anyone." *Except me, when it's done*, she failed to add.

"I admire that in you."

"What?" She spread her fingers across his chest.

"Your absolute fearlessness to jump into any fire. It's not that you're reckless. You're not at all. You know the consequences—you're not unmindful. It's not even that you don't care. It's that you want this one thing more than you fear the fallout. I wish I could be that way."

Kentucky didn't know what to say. It was almost as if she'd forgotten that he saw her—really saw her.

He always had.

Everyone else outside their circle thought she was just the wild girl who swilled shine from the wrong side of the tracks.

That was a gift beyond gold.

"You are that way. I didn't jump alone."

"No, I tripped on and fell into the fire." His hand stroked down her back. "But it burns so good, baby."

"Will you be here when I wake up?"

"Do you want me to be?"

"Yes." She snuggled closer. "If I didn't, I'd tell you to make me a sandwich on your way out."

He laughed and kissed her forehead.

They lay in the silent dark together in the cocoon they'd made for themselves for a long time before either of them slept.

7

SEAN WOKE HER up with a hot cup of coffee under her nose.

"You know the way to my heart," she mumbled, and accepted the cup gratefully.

"Drink up, Tuck. I have a day planned."

"The whole day?" She grinned. "What about work?"

"Fuck it." He flashed her a crooked grin. "Actually, I didn't think about that. Do you have stuff you need to get done for the shop?"

"I do." She nodded. "But I'll accept your day and raise you this evening. You can help me finish up some of the regular maintenance work."

"What makes you think I know how to do that?"

"Oh, please. You don't learn to fly Black Hawks and have no idea how to work on them. You can change the oil in the '12 Jeep Grand Cherokee."

"Yeah, I suppose I can, at that."

"Unless you don't want to?" She watched him over her cup.

"I could use some time in my own head with busy hands, you know? I'm looking forward to it."

"So what's your plan? What's our lovely day?"

His eyes suddenly darkened and his gaze was centered squarely on her breasts. The sheet had fallen down and she was bare to his view.

"It's going to be a lovely day in bed if you don't put on some clothes."

"I could go for that." She grinned and took another sip of coffee, not bothering to cover herself up.

"Woman," he teased.

"Fine." She supposed he was right. She was a little sore, but it was the most delicious feeling. "Where are we going?"

"I guess that all depends if you still have that Harley in storage."

"You're not driving my Harley."

"No, you are. I'll hop on back."

She arched a brow. "Really?"

"What, like I have a problem with a woman who can handle her machine? It takes nothing away from me. Your hands will be on the bars and mine, well… I'll be free to put them where I like."

She laughed. "You better be careful. You don't want to distract me too much."

"Maybe I do. Maybe my plan is to get you on some deserted country road and do bad things to you in the light of day."

"Then I guess you better pack a blanket. I don't want burrs or chiggers." She got up and padded toward the shower.

"I'm one step ahead of you. I even packed a picnic."

She turned on the water and let the spray fall over her. "So you thought of everything."

"One does try."

"One does succeed." She soaped up and exhaled as the hot water soothed her aching muscles and helped clear her head.

"Screw it," she heard him mumble.

His hands reached through the shower curtain and took the soap from her. "We've got time."

Soap-slicked fingers moved over her shoulders, down her spine and around her waist.

Her breath caught in her throat. "Sean."

"No, you don't like this?" He continued his ministrations, the tone of his voice making it obvious he knew full well what he was doing to her.

"I thought you wanted to take the bike out."

"Just imagine what we could do on the bike." His hands moved down the outside of her thighs and back up the inside, only for him to swoop down to her knees again. "How much would it take to distract you enough to make you pull over? Do you think I could fuck you on that bike at seventy miles per hour?"

"I think that it's a pretty fantasy, but the reality would be awkward and deadly."

"Fine, then let me drive."

"You're driving now." That familiar burn started between her legs and all she could think about was getting him to touch her there.

"The wind on our faces, while we laugh at death

and drink down every moment, suck the marrow dry from this world."

She shivered with both anticipation and pleasure. That was exactly how she wanted to live her life.

She and Sean were more alike than she'd ever thought. "Indeed, you are a poet."

"No, I just know what I want."

Kentucky licked her lips. "Do you? Are you sure about that?"

He stripped off his clothes and climbed into the shower with her, his skin hotter than the water that sluiced over them. She took the soap and lathered it in her hands as he had done and returned the favor, smoothing her hands all over the wide expanse of his chest, his shoulders, his back.

Then she moved her hands down over his hips and his thighs, returning the teasing, taunting caress.

His cock was hard and at attention.

He seemed indefatigable. She wondered if they really could spend the whole day in bed. She rinsed the soap off her hands and reached for him, closed her fingers around the hard velvet length of him.

Kentucky had never imagined he'd be here with her like this. That wasn't to say she hadn't fantasized about it, but in the real? These things didn't happen to her.

She had to remember that they were happening to her, right now. Kentucky had to keep reminding herself to live these moments like any other—living them to make a memory to let her surrender to the moment.

Or to what she knew was inevitable.

The low growl of gratification in the back of his

throat anchored her in the moment. She knelt down, the fine spray of water at her back and over her shoulders.

He pushed his hand through her damp hair and she took him into her mouth, relishing not only the feel of him, the sounds of his pleasure, but the power she had over him. Not because she could deny him bliss, but because she could give it to him.

It occurred to her, not for the first time, that he was indeed a beautiful specimen of manhood. She loved his oblique muscles the most—those hard lines often referred to as an Adonis apron, smooth lines of muscle that seemed to point straight toward his cock.

His legs were strong and powerful, thickly muscled, just like everything else on him. In his youth, he'd been a kind of young god, but now he was earthier, harder.

God, so much harder.

Everywhere.

Everything she touched was like living marble. This was a man built for fighting, for killing—for saving. His shoulders were just broad enough to handle the hero's mantle.

She looked up and met his eyes. Kentucky loved that about the way they joined. It wasn't some fey, wispy sort of lovemaking. Some pretty, lacy ideal. It was intense, primal...and he wasn't afraid to look into her eyes.

Kentucky pressed her nails lightly into his glutes, pulled him forward. She sheathed him with her mouth, his flesh silky and hot against her tongue.

"Sweet Christ, Kentucky..."

She continued the campaign, bobbing down his

length, tasting him, swirling her tongue over the thick topography of his flesh.

"I'm already close," he warned.

She replaced her mouth with her hand, stroking him slowly, making it last. "Come for me, Sean. I want to taste you."

He'd braced himself with one hand on the shower-curtain rod, the other on the safety handle in the shower. His knuckles whitened as he tightened his grip. Every muscle in his body seemed to be flexed as he fought the sensation, fought the tidal wave.

She wondered how far she could push him, how high?

Kentucky slowed her strokes but then brought him to her lips, where she teased the crown of his manhood with her tongue, licking and laving, changing her technique and increasing pressure depending on that delicious growl that kept reverberating from him.

"You're killing me."

"That is why they call it the little death." She took him deep again.

His body spasmed and he arched toward her, hips thrusting, and she felt only satisfaction when he found his completion.

"Shit." He turned the water off.

She looked up to see that he held the shower curtain, rod and all, in his hand. He'd pulled it down with the strain of his orgasm.

Kentucky grinned. "I'm so the boss of you."

"I will fix this before I leave."

She laughed. "I'm kind of proud of it."

He lifted her up as if she were no bigger than a doll. "But now turnabout is only fair play. I think you're in for some quid pro quo."

She squirmed, delighted at the idea. "Well, if you insist."

"I do insist." He wrapped a towel around her. "Bed?"

"Definitely."

Sean carried her into the bedroom and perched her on the edge of the bed. "Spread for me. Show me."

She spread her legs wide and he knelt between them, pushing her back on the mess of blankets on the bed.

Kentucky leaned back and stared up at the ceiling, fisting the duvet as she waited for the onslaught of sensation.

God, but he was amazing.

He kissed her there first. His lips soft and warm, a gentle press before he slipped his tongue inside her and traced the seam back up to her clit.

"You taste so good."

"So do you," she replied, anticipating the next onslaught.

His fingers pushed inside her while his tongue worked at the swollen bud and waves of sensation echoed through her body.

He played her as if she were some sort of delicate instrument and he a master composer. It was nothing short of bliss.

She found her hips bucking, driving her cleft up against his mouth. He'd gripped her hips, pinning her where he wanted her. His breath was a warm caress over the heated and engorged flesh when he spoke. "When

I'm done here, when you're coming and riding the wave, I'm going to kiss you and we'll taste each other."

It was naughty and decadent, and it caused her interior walls to constrict around his fingers.

"Like that, do you? Yeah, me, too. I want to know what we taste like together."

He dipped his head again, suckling and thrusting.

Just as he'd promised, when she was riding his fingers and arching up into her orgasm, he broke away and slammed his mouth into hers.

They tasted sweet together, a comingling of evidence of their ecstasy.

When she lay sated and exhausted, he slapped her ass lightly. "Okay, rest time is over. Let's go."

"What? I thought we were spending the day inside."

"No, that was just a good start to an even better day."

She licked her lips.

"Stop that," he said. "It makes me think about your pretty lips on my cock. And we just can't do that again." Sean grinned. "I need like fifteen minutes."

Her interior walls tensed at the idea, but holy hell. She wasn't used to this much activity. "I think I need more than fifteen minutes."

"Okay, that might have been optimistic on my part, as well. But the will is there." He nodded.

"I say we put a moratorium on it at least until tonight."

"So we definitely need to get out of the house or I'm just going to have to bury my face between those pretty thighs again."

"And I'd let you, even though I'd be sorry for it later."

"So where's the bike?"

"It's in the bay with my personal vehicles."

"How many do you have?" He raised a brow.

"Oh, you know how I am with the project cars. I always have at least three or four. Then I sell 'em."

He got dressed and laced into his combat boots while she searched for something clean to wear. She found a pair of black jeans and an old band T-shirt from high school, then pulled on her own combat boots. Of course, hers hadn't seen any actual combat. They were Doc Martens. She tied her wet hair up into a low ponytail.

"Except Betty."

"I might sell Betty."

"You lie. You've put off finishing her just so you don't have to make that choice."

"You don't know everything, Mr. Smarty-Pants."

"Not everything, Kentucky. But I do know you."

"As if, bro," she teased. "So, you still cool to let me drive?"

"It's your bike." He grabbed her. "Let's go to that little coffee shop in Ozawkie for breakfast."

"I haven't thought about that place in years. I wonder if they're still open."

"I Googled. They have crepes…"

"Done."

8

IT HAD BEEN a long time since Sean had been on the road like this.

A long time since he'd felt the wind rushing around him, the connection to the pavement, the endless possibilities of everywhere the road could take him.

He felt a lot like this when he was in the air. He loved flying the Black Hawks, but there was something more intimate about being on a bike, having all of that power between his legs.

Sean especially liked being on the back of the bike, with his arms wrapped around Kentucky's waist, feeling her powerful body holding up the bike, guiding it down the spinning ribbon of highway. Feeling her ass pressed up against him.

He liked the freedom he felt with her driving, too.

He could race with the wind and he didn't have to be in control. He wasn't the one whose hand was the guiding force of life and death.

Although it was a little terrifying, too. He was so

used to having all of that responsibility resting on his shoulders. It was quite something to surrender it to someone else.

To put his life in her hands.

Even though she was an expert rider.

He watched the speedometer as it kept climbing, and the higher it got, the faster they flew, the less it mattered to him that he wasn't in control.

Sean was flying, defying gravity while still cruising the ground. The sky loomed ever larger, brighter, calling him.

He couldn't imagine ever doing this with Lynnie.

He felt guilty for the thought, but then it was gone. He had no reason to feel guilty, at least not for this. There were things she'd enjoyed and things she hadn't. She and Kentucky were two different people.

Lynnie was gone.

He and Kentucky had been left behind.

So now they were living the life that had been given to them. What was so wrong with that? It wasn't as if they were pretending she'd never been. Or they hadn't both loved her.

He tightened his arm around her waist and inhaled the sweet apple scent of her hair.

It wasn't long before they pulled into the parking lot for the tiny coffee shop out in the middle of the country-side called The Ruby Slipper.

It was an odd place to open a coffeehouse and it had been expected to fail. But the kids from Lawrence who didn't want anything so mainstream as a coffee shop in town would come hang out and read poetry late into the night. They'd drive out to where there was no internet and barely any cell service and have poetry slams and study nights and drink their own weight in coffee.

He held the door open for her and she ordered them two coffees and two apple fritters. Sean certainly wasn't going to complain.

The fritter was warm and flaky, the apples inside sweet with just a bit of cinnamon. It practically melted on his tongue and it was good. Not just that the fritter tasted good, but everything about this moment was good.

The burn of the coffee, the scent in the air and the woman sitting across from him with the sun shining down on her like a halo.

It was a lovely image, but he wasn't trying to make her into a saint or a maiden in distress. He was pretty sure Kentucky Lee was the dragon in that story.

Sean wasn't sure who he was, but he was okay with that for now.

"This is the best morning I've had in a long time," she said while taking a sip of her coffee out of the fat red cappuccino mug.

"Me, too." He took another sip of his own coffee.

For a second, just that single instant, he wondered what it would be like to wake up to her—to this—every day. He'd never wanted to stay in Winchester, but it suddenly wasn't about the geography.

It was about the players.

It was about looking at a beautiful woman who was everything he wished he could be. It was about the taste of the coffee and the tightness in his chest when he thought about leaving.

It was about how when he was with her, he wasn't drowning. How he could breathe.

Hell, he could even float.

Maybe even fly.

How had he missed it? There was nothing about Kentucky that was a shackle, an anchor or a weight. Not the way he'd felt with Lynnie.

Guilt surged again.

"I hate to ask that basic girl question, but what are you thinking about?"

He arched a brow.

She laughed. "It's just, there was this look of joy on your face and then it was like a storm cloud blotted out your sun."

"I was thinking about Lynnie."

"What were you thinking about her? Tell me?" She reached out and squeezed his hand.

He searched her eyes. No, he didn't want to tell her those things. He didn't know what good they would do. "I was thinking about the last time we came here."

"Did she read one of her poems?"

"She did. It was about beginnings. Endings. And how they don't mean what we think they do."

"I'm sorry I missed that."

"Me, too." He exhaled. "I miss her, Kentucky."

"I know."

"I think I'll always miss her, but it's different somehow, you know?"

She didn't speak but instead took another drink of her coffee.

"But this isn't about Lynnie today."

"No? What's it about?"

"Us." He nodded. "Who we are. And like you said, we're not dead."

"I like that." She popped a bite of fritter into her mouth. "So what else is on your agenda? The picnic? Motorcycle sex?"

"Definitely the picnic. What about a ride in a puddle jumper?"

"Seriously? Yes!"

When he was a kid, he'd seen those tiny planes called puddle jumpers, sometimes used as crop dusters, in the air. He'd never thought they seemed like a good idea. Even as a pilot, he was amazed at how the science worked to keep those things in the air.

But she was always ready for an adventure.

She'd shown him what she could do; he'd seen Betty, her garage. Now it was his turn. He didn't know why this was suddenly so important to him, but it was. Almost as much as the next breath he took.

She crammed the rest of the fritter into her mouth and downed the coffee. "Let's go. I'm ready."

He laughed and finished his pastry. "Yeah, okay. Slow down."

"Nope. Can't do that. I might miss something important."

"Okay, boss. Take us to the Lawrence Municipal Airport. The little jumper is waiting for us."

Back on the bike, in no time at all she was speeding down single-lane highways through cornfields to get to the small airport.

When she slowed to a stop and took off her helmet,

she asked, "So how did you get a plane on such short notice?"

"Buddy of mine. His family uses one for short trips down to Texas and Oklahoma for cattle auctions. I told him I was in town and had a pretty girl to impress."

She blushed. "You did not."

"I did."

"You don't ever have to impress me, Sean." She looked down at her boots, seeming to be suddenly shy.

He tilted her chin up with his thumb. "Any man you let into your bed better always be trying to impress you."

"You're silly."

"Hey, I'm not kidding." The thought of any other man trying to impress her hit all his buttons. But he knew that wasn't his place.

"So where are you taking me?"

"Where do you want to go?"

"I want to see the Chalk Pyramids. Can we go that far?"

"Yeah, I'll make sure we have enough fuel. It'll take about an hour, give or take."

"Really?" She grinned.

"If that's what you want. I've never seen them either. It sounds like fun."

The small plane was painted red and had his friend's ranch's logo painted onto the side so it looked as if it had been branded into it. He did the walk-through with the attendant, made sure it had enough fuel to get them where they wanted to go and home, and registered the flight plan with the tower.

He double-checked their safety gear and made sure she had a headset so they could talk over the noise during the flight.

She squealed when they took off and he found it to be incredibly endearing.

The higher the craft climbed, the more she oohed, aahed and pointed at various things she noticed.

He liked how she saw the world. How she processed things.

The landscape began to change. As they left behind the countryside of eastern Kansas—slightly hilly due to glacial till and proximity to the Ozarks—the land started to level out, conforming to what one would expect of Kansas terrain. Flat and endless. But it had its own beauty, from the endless rolling waves of wheat and corn to the green of the Flint Hills dotted with cattle.

It wasn't long before the Chalk Pyramids, or Monument Rocks, came into view. They looked as if they belonged in Arizona or Nevada rather than Kansas.

Some standing at seventy feet tall, they formed buttes and arches, like strange tributes to ancient peoples.

"I always wanted to see these. I don't know why I didn't just get in Betty and drive here," she said through the mic, her voice tinged with what he thought was awe.

"Yeah, but this view is much better. Want to get closer?"

"Yes!"

He took the little plane down and circled around the chalk formations, gliding as slowly as he dared to let her have the best view.

"They're so powerful. Look at them, just standing

there impervious to time. To the landscape around them. They don't fit here, but they stand there anyway." She laughed. "Kind of like me, I guess. I mean, I don't know how powerful I am, but I don't fit in Winchester. Yet I stand there."

"You fit anywhere you want to be, Tuck."

She was quiet and kept her own counsel on the flight back to Lawrence.

When they were on the ground and he'd helped her out of the plane, she launched herself into his arms.

"Thank you."

"My pleasure." He enjoyed having her in his arms. It was a simple thing to have done for her, really. He couldn't help but think Lynnie wouldn't have wanted to do this with him either. He could never get her to go up with him.

Yeah, he was a different man than the boy who'd been quarterback for the Winchester Eagles. A million miles away from that kid.

"I'm starved. That fritter didn't go very far."

"Good. Picnic time."

"Oh, is the food going to be okay?"

"Yeah, it's in a cooler in your top box." He pointed to the rear of the bike.

"Trust the flyboy to be prepared for any emergency."

"Of course. I know better than to take risks with not feeding you. Your hangry self is terrifying."

She shoved his shoulder lightly. "So where are we going for our picnic?"

"Do you remember that road...?"

"Oh God, yes!"

He loved that she knew what he was thinking. It was as if they were always on the same wavelength.

"I'll let you drive," she said, handing him the keys to the Harley.

"Hell yeah!" He swung his leg over the bike and she climbed on behind him, palms flat on his stomach. It felt good to have her hands on him—hell, everything about this day was good.

The road he was taking her to was one where they'd gotten lost heading into Lawrence for a party on a Saturday night. They'd finally given up and had their own party. It had been their junior year, and Sean and Lynnie had been broken up.

It took him a while to find the right turnoff. It was a tiny road, gravel and unkempt, but there was a hunting platform in the trees and they'd climbed up there and partied until dawn.

He carried the cooler and hoisted himself onto the platform, checking its durability before allowing Kentucky to come up.

He had a bottle of sparkling grape juice since they were driving, cheese and apples, cold roasted chicken breast, and a Godiva chocolate bar for her for dessert.

Sean handed her a paper plate and she piled it high. He liked that about her, too. She was never shy with her food, and she never pretended she didn't want to eat if she was hungry.

"That night has to be on my list of wildest times ever," she said. "It was all of us, right? And some new people? Lynnie's boyfriend at the time and some of his friends?"

He remembered that night so clearly. He'd been tempted to get drunk, like some of the other people in their group. But he'd felt as if he had to be responsible. Someone should be able to drive if they needed it, but it had been hard. He'd just wanted to drown his feelings in a bottle of that cheap shine Kentucky had made in her aunt's bathtub.

"Yeah, everyone was there."

"I remember vaguely that you were shooting the new BF dagger glares all night?"

"Do you? What else do you remember?"

She gave him a crooked grin. "I remember eating way too many of those moonshine cherries. I still love those things. God, but my head felt like there was a whole marching band in there the next morning. It was ridiculous."

"How much trouble were you in?"

"None. My aunt said my hangover was my punishment. That and making me watch VHS recordings of old black-and-white big band shows with her."

"I guess you learned your lesson."

"I did." She laughed. "I still love those damn cherries, but I know my limit. I can't remember a lot of what happened."

"Really? Would you like me to tell you?" His eyes focused on her lips, those soft, lovely lips that had been wrapped around his cock earlier that morning.

"I don't know. What did I do?" She looked horrified. "No one said anything to me. How bad is it?"

"No one saw but me."

"Oh Jesus." She put her hand over her face. "You

might as well tell me. My not knowing doesn't change what happened."

"You saw how pissed I was and when Lynnie and that guy climbed down to go 'for a walk,' you cornered me. Wouldn't let me follow them."

"And?" She bit her lip.

"And you told me there were more girls in the world than Lynnie James."

"Oh, I did not." Her eyes widened. "Did I?"

"Oh, yeah." He laughed. "You said that Lynnie was amazing and beautiful, but there were other amazing and beautiful girls. Then you laid one on me."

"Laid one? You mean I *kissed* you?" She laughed. "No way. You're just playing with me now."

"I am most certainly not. It happened. Right there." He pointed to the corner of the platform. "You backed me up against that branch right there."

Kentucky scrubbed a hand down her face. "Oh my God."

"Look, I always figured it was just the cherries. At first I thought you were just trying to make me feel better."

"Did it work?"

"Yeah, momentarily. Until I realized you were hammered."

"Well, I'm thoroughly embarrassed."

"Don't be. We were kids."

"I'm also irritated that I can't remember it. It would have saved me a lot of angst." She covered her mouth. "Forget I said that part."

"Why?"

"Because it's gross."

"Gross? How? You think I never saw how you looked at me?"

"Oh, let's not do this."

"Why not? You were talking about intimacy earlier. A connection. It goes both ways."

"I have to confess my pathetic teen crush? That's more embarrassing than laying a kiss on you at some impromptu party in the sticks."

"Fine. I'll make a confession of my own. It wasn't the way Lynnie looked at me that made me want to be a better man. It was you."

She looked as if he'd struck her. "What do you mean?" Her voice was practically a whisper.

"Lynnie could see the good in everyone. That was one of her gifts. But not you. You always saw the darkness—you saw every contingency and prepared. For death, betrayal. But that didn't stop you from letting people in. But the way you looked at me..." He shook his head. "Christ, Kentucky. You made me feel like I was a hundred feet tall and could carry the weight of the world as if it was nothing more than a gym bag. I wanted to earn that. Be worthy of it. I guess in a way, when I was deciding between college and enlisting, I enlisted because I wanted to be worthy of that from you. If I was worthy in your eyes, I'd be good enough for Lynnie, too."

9

KENTUCKY'S EMOTIONS WELLED over her like a typhoon.

She'd always known that he saw her, who she was, but she hadn't realized she'd had that kind of impact on him and what he'd chosen to do with his life.

If she were the kind to lay guilt on her own doorstep, she could blame herself for his split with Lynnie. Only she wasn't that sort and Sean was a grown man who'd made his own decisions. She'd never interfered with their relationship.

Even this kiss they were talking about, it had happened while they were broken up.

"Sean, you could never be anything but worthy."

"I'm not so sure, but thanks for believing it."

"Well, I am sure. So that's all you need to know."

She wondered why he'd brought her here, the significance. He'd obviously planned the whole day. He was taking them around to the stomping ground of their youth. This place didn't have any super significance, or it hadn't until he told her that she'd kissed him here.

Part of her wished that she could remember it, and the other part, not so much. She was glad she hadn't had to fret about having kissed her best friend's ex-boyfriend, or fret about it once more when they started dating again.

"Ready to go?" It was his turn to change the subject.

"Yeah, but where are we going now?"

"Swimming at Mossy Rock."

She grinned. "Yeah, but whatever will I wear?"

"I actually thought ahead. I packed your swimming suit."

He really had gone all out. "Wow, okay. You thought of everything."

They cleaned up the remains of their picnic and packed their trash in the cooler to dispose of it back at her place. Then they were on the road again and she was driving.

He'd taken her flying; now it was her turn to take him—only they were flying on the open road.

She liked feeling his strong body pressed against hers, liked that he didn't have some weird machismo bullshit about riding on the back with her. Liked that this whole day had been about the two of them together.

There was a small part of her that was glad he was leaving, that this was temporary. Maybe she didn't know exactly when he was leaving, but it helped to know that he was. That knowledge in the back of her mind was like a wall, keeping her safe. Because she could get used to this, she could let herself want this, but even if he wasn't leaving to go back to his post, he'd leave to go on missions. She'd never know if he

was coming home or not, even if he wanted that kind
of future with her.

Kentucky was a lot of things, but she knew her own
weaknesses. After everyone she'd lost, she couldn't
invest her whole heart in someone who lived that kind
of life.

Hell, what was she thinking about, anyway? He
didn't want a commitment. They'd agreed. She hated
that she had to keep warning herself of that. Maybe she
wasn't as grown-up as she thought she was.

Maybe this was about more than grief for her. This
was about fulfilling a teen fantasy that she hadn't
known she still needed. Only Sean Dryden wasn't the
golden boy, she kept reminding herself. He wasn't a boy
at all but a man. Damaged and hurting.

She flung those thoughts to the side of the road and
increased the bike's speed, causing her heart to beat
faster, the blood to rush through her veins as the thrill
bloomed through her.

It seemed like only a second until she had to slow so
that they could creep down the dirt path on the opposite
side of Mossy Rock. This took them right through the
farmer's land, but he didn't seem to be anywhere in sight.

Not that he'd have said anything. They weren't kids
anymore.

It seemed that Eric and Rachel were of the same
mind. They were currently in the middle of the pond,
splashing each other just like when they were kids.

Kentucky took off her helmet and waved.

Rachel waved back and Eric took that opportunity

to lunge for her and push her under the water. She came up spluttering, cursing, with the promise of retribution.

"Looks like they had the same idea," she said.

"No, I told them to come. All of us together, like old times. Eddie's was good, but it was grown-up us. Here we can be kids again."

"I'll change into my suit."

"Can I watch?"

"With Eric and Rachel here?"

"What they don't know won't hurt them." He flashed her an evil grin.

"So that's how we're going to play it." She nodded slowly and with an evil grin of her own. "You just wait."

Kentucky sauntered over to the "changing bushes" where everyone used to get dressed and slipped into her pink bikini, then bounded toward the water.

She dove right in, the water just the right temperature. Of course, when night fell, if they stayed that long, she'd be freezing her ass off again.

Kentucky thought about that first night here, them together.

No matter what happened between them now, Mossy Rock would always mean something else to her. Those memories of that night would be superimposed on everything else.

Rachel didn't hesitate to hug first Sean and then her. "I'm so glad you asked us to come. Eric and I have been here all day. We even cooked out." She nodded over to the sandy beach and the small fire pit.

"Did you save any for me?" Kentucky asked, rubbing her stomach.

Rachel narrowed her eyes. "Sean said you guys already ate."

"I did. It was delicious. But you know I can't resist a crispy hot dog."

Eric laughed. "Yeah, I saved you two. They're on the spit."

"Extra well-done?"

"Practically charred," he answered.

"You love me." She smiled.

"You know I do." Eric used Rachel's inattention to grab her yet again and submerge her in the water.

When Rachel came back up, she said, "I don't know how I stand you."

"Yeah, me neither." He kissed her forehead. "But I'm lucky you do."

"And don't you forget it."

Kentucky watched the moment play out between them as she stuffed a hot dog in her mouth. He was right—it was practically charred. It was just the way she loved them. She wasn't actually hungry, but the memories that came with this place, with burned hot dogs and long summer evenings with friends, whet her appetite.

Her emotion suddenly choked her. No matter what she did to store up these memories, no matter how many times she unfolded the quilt of moments to touch it, sense it, feel it, they would never be the same again because Lynnie was gone.

She wasn't coming back.

It wasn't just that her memories were different. The whole world was different.

Tears welled hot and acidic in her eyes and she inhaled deeply to center herself, to keep those traitorous tears from falling.

"Hey, you okay?" Rachel had come up onto the beach next to her.

"No, not really."

"Lynnie." Rachel nodded. "It's weird to be here without her."

"More than you know."

Rachel put a hand on her shoulder meant to comfort her and they both turned to watch the guys in the water. "I'm glad they're getting time together. Eric's missed him a lot. Been worried about him."

"He seems to be doing better than he was." Or maybe it was just because he spent all of his time between her legs. People couldn't, or shouldn't, be sad when they were having that much sex.

"Where did you guys go today?" Rachel asked.

"We made a day of it. We had breakfast at The Ruby Slipper, he took me up in a plane to show off his piloting skills, then lunch at that old hunting place... Remember that?"

"So you were really making the rounds, huh? It kind of seems like he's letting go."

She supposed that he was. Kentucky got the feeling that he was saying goodbye. He was giving her something pretty to store away in her memory box with the rest of them.

Kentucky knew it was ending, but she'd sort of expected him to spend all of his leave with her. They'd never talked about it.

"I guess that's a good thing." It was. She didn't want

him to hold on to his guilt or his pain. She wanted him to be whole, healthy and happy.

"Yeah." Rachel hugged her again. "You going to eat that other hot dog? If not, that bad boy is mine."

"I wasn't even really hungry. But you know, we come to Mossy Rock, we need hot dogs."

"Memory taste," Rachel agreed. "I know what you mean." She picked up the last hot dog with two fingers and took a tiny bite.

Then she looked out at Eric and made sure he could see her before stuffing as much of the hot dog as she could into her mouth. Kentucky could almost swear Eric could hear the audible snap of teeth as she bit down on her mouthful, because he cringed and Rachel smiled sweet as that apple fritter she'd had earlier.

"Well, aren't you just diabolical."

"He kept dunking me. He needs to learn that the only thing that's changed between us is our relationship status on Facebook. Just because I happen to be a little bit enamored with his smile and…other things… that doesn't mean I won't crush him like a bug the way I used to when he'd get out of line."

Kentucky laughed. "Yeah, it's good that some things never change."

"It really is. I thought that being with Eric might mean the end of us. But it was honestly a natural progression." She looked around. "I wish I had something else to put in my mouth to taunt him."

Kentucky found herself smiling again. It was true— nothing really had changed. They were always together, they loved to give each other what for, and it was as though becoming a couple had completed something between them. That things were now the way they were always supposed to be.

"I think you've taunted him enough."

"No, not nearly. If it were you, you'd still be making him pay. Don't try to say you wouldn't."

It made her think about Sean. "Yeah, you're so right."

She thought about all the ways she wanted to taunt him and keep taunting him. Although she couldn't forget what Rachel had said about Sean letting go.

She was right.

It was as if today, even though it had been fun, was a kind of pilgrimage. That could only mean goodbye, but like the old adage said, you never could really go home.

Which ultimately meant that her time with Sean was drawing to a close.

Kentucky looked out across the water at him, the familiar silhouette of his shoulders, the lines of muscle down his back, the thickly muscled forearms and the way the sun glinted off blond hair.

She prepared her heart to let go, too.

He turned and saw her scrutiny and gave her a smile that she somehow knew was only for her. A kind of sweet acknowledgment of this time they'd shared.

She'd remember him like that forever.

"Hey, you disappeared on me again," Rachel said.

"Yeah, I seem to be doing that a lot lately."

"You ready to tell me about what happened with you two?"

"Nope."

"Come on. I'm dying to know. So is Eric."

"Well, that's not weird at all. Sean's dead ex-fiancée's brother wants to know all about the new girl he's banging?"

"So you admit that you're having sex?" Rachel winked, but then seeing Kentucky's scowl, she backed off a bit. "Eric and I both just want you guys to be happy. What better way than all of us together?"

Kentucky raised a brow.

"That sounded way dirtier than I meant it. You know what I mean. Whenever we're together, some part of Lynnie will always live on."

"Yeah, see? That's the problem. I don't want to be a vehicle to resurrect the dead. I don't want to be a second choice. I don't want to have her hanging between us. And she would. I loved Lynnie. You know that. But I don't want the ghost of her in my bed."

Rachel nodded. "I understand that. But I don't think it would be that way."

Kentucky shook her head. "I'm not her. I can't be her."

"No one wants you to be."

"I'm the bad girl, the rebel with too many causes."

"No, you're not. Not anymore. You run your own business, you're responsible… Everyone knows you and respects you."

"Girl like me, we don't end up with men like Sean Dryden."

"Why not?"

Yeah, why not? her brain demanded. Why didn't they? She was just as good as anyone else. And Sean himself had changed.

She kept thinking about a life and a future. A family.

If she had those things, would she really want them with a man who, every time he left the house to do his job, every time he was called away on a mission, would put her on tenterhooks? Would she always be waiting for that call that could come, the one where they told her that the fairy tale was over and he was dead, too?

She just couldn't risk it.

She was a daredevil because she wanted to wring every second out of life and all the bounty it had to offer. But at some point, she knew herself. She'd start wishing for the call because she wanted to get it over with, because that was how her own story always unfolded.

God, but she could be so morbid sometimes.

"I can't talk about this anymore."

"Maybe you should talk about it with him, Kentucky. The way he keeps watching you, he's not trying to hide anything that happened, the way things have changed between you."

"So when are you and Eric getting married?" She flipped the tables on her friend.

"Oh, hell. Not you, too."

"What do you mean?" Kentucky took no small amount of glee in harassing her friend. She knew that Rachel's mother had been pestering them to get engaged and set a date. Her mom was super old-school and thought they should be married instead of living together.

"You know very well what I mean. She's started in on grandchildren. Grandchildren! Do I look like I'm ready to start having babies? Eric and I don't even know if we want kids. We just want to enjoy each other right now and let things happen as they will. I'm sure we'll get married eventually, but we want to do it in our own time. Not because my mother wouldn't stop meddling."

Kentucky felt a rush of sympathy for Rachel's mom. "If my mother were still alive, I'd get married tomorrow if that was the trade-off."

"To Sean or Eric?" Rachel teased.

"I don't care. Whatever would make her happy and keep her with me. I'd marry you if it would do the trick." Kentucky grinned at her.

"Ha, you should be so lucky."

"I should. So would Eric."

"He's proud. He lost his parents, his sister. I know he's feeling a little bit like the world might be against us. You know, like it's a chink in his armor for him to love someone so thoroughly."

"So he wants to pop the question, but he's afraid."

"Maybe a little. Like as soon as he admits he wants me forever, something will take me away." Rachel shook her head.

"You know, I understand that. I really do. I feel a little bit like that, too."

"Complicated things, my friend. I mean, I can't promise nothing will ever happen to me. Anything can happen to any of us. Everything that we think is a guarantee isn't. Nothing is absolute. I wish I could change that for both of you. Maybe you're luckier because you know that."

"Maybe," Kentucky agreed. "But I'd love to have no idea that's how things work. I'd love to— No, you know what? That's not true. I don't feel that way at all." She had some things she needed to think about.

"Are you guys going to talk the rest of the day away or come swim?" Sean waded over to them.

They frolicked, splashed and laughed until dark, when they went their separate ways. Once they were back at Kentucky's place, Sean said, "So was today a good day?"

"Yeah, you totally thought of everything. It was like all the old times became new."

"It was like healing balm for me, to replace old memories of those places with new ones. Even if the old memories were good."

"Yeah." She nodded. "The best memories are layered things with different depths and textures that all come together to make a certain whole."

"Exactly that." He pulled her into his strong embrace, resting his chin on the top of her head.

She felt so safe, so warm and for one horrible minute as if that was exactly where she belonged. Horrible because that just wasn't possible. Sean Dryden couldn't be her idea of home.

"Can I stay?" he asked.

"Yeah. You can stay until your leave is over." She turned her cheek against his shoulder. "If you want."

"I'd like that."

10

SEAN DRYDEN HAD started to feel a sense of contentment and peace that he'd never had. And it was all thanks to Kentucky. As much as he believed he needed to be worthy of the way that she looked at him, he didn't feel as if he had to be something he wasn't when he was with her. He felt that if he gave his best for her, for himself, then it was enough.

It was a strange dichotomy that made him want to be better, be more, even though he felt as though his self was enough.

His guilt about Lynnie had started to fade ever so slowly.

Being with Kentucky wasn't the only factor. Spending time with Eric and Rachel, coming back to Winchester, and exorcising all the old haunts had helped, too.

The first time he'd spoken to Eric after Lynnie died…the first thing he'd said was "It's not your fault." That had been a knife that twisted so deep in his gut he hadn't known if he'd ever be able to dig it out. Now, instead of a wound or a weapon, it was a balm.

He was so grateful that he hadn't lost his friendship with Eric, too. If Eric had blamed him, he'd never have gotten over it.

Kentucky felt so good in his arms that he wanted to keep her there.

He started wondering what it would be like to have her for always, not just for now. Except he knew that wouldn't be fair to her, not with his current job.

His phone started buzzing on the nightstand. He could see from the caller ID that it was his commanding officer.

Yeah, for exactly this reason. This was why it wouldn't be fair to her.

He untangled himself from the warm, sweet woman in his arms and answered.

"Dryden, you've been recalled."

"Yes, sir."

"Report to Fort Leavenworth. And, Dryden?"

"Yeah?"

"Move your ass. Shit went south and it went south bad on an op in Colombia. It's not a rescue mission, because there are no survivors."

"Yes, sir."

A knot tightened in his gut. He knew the mission he was talking about. This group of guerrillas had just called down a wholesale slaughter on themselves.

He looked down at Kentucky and scrawled her a note. She deserved better than a note on her pillow, but he didn't have time for anything else.

Sean got dressed and took one last look at Kentucky before he headed back to the motel where he'd left his gear.

He looked at his phone to check the time after he packed up the few things he had scattered across the room. It was 3:00 a.m. He texted Eric to see if he was awake.

His phone rang shortly after.

"Yeah, I'm awake," Eric said. "What's up? You okay?"

"I just got recalled. My leave is over."

"Thought you had another week?"

"I was supposed to have another three."

"Shit, what happened?"

"Classified. But needless to say, I'm going. I don't want to leave Kentucky vulnerable. That girl deserves more from me than a note on her pillow."

"Probably," Eric agreed. "How can I help?"

"Can you tell her that I was recalled? I mean, I left it in the note, but that feels like such a shitty thing to do."

"You could wake her up."

"And spill my guts all over her about how I don't want to leave her, make her worry? I'd see the look in her eyes and want her to know I'd do anything not to see it. You know?"

"Yeah, man. I do know. I really do," Eric said. "I'll tell her if I think she needs to hear it. But you and Kentucky have never been in the habit of lying to each other. So I'm sure she'll take your note at face value."

"We might have something, Eric."

"Might? After I saw the way you two were looking

at each other, there's no doubt in my mind you have something. But if it's a real something, it'll still be there when you get back."

"I don't know about that. Timing is everything."

"Sean?"

"Yeah?"

"Take care, brother."

"As much as I can."

"Your enlistment is coming up, isn't it?"

"What does that matter?"

"I'm getting out."

"Why?" Such a thing sounded so foreign to him. Sean was army for life. He loved his job. Loved what he did. He thought Eric did, too.

"I've already got the approval from the Department of Defense to be an independent contractor."

"You mean mercenary?"

"Yeah. I'm starting my own company. I want you to come work for me. I need a pilot. The money is better and the benefits will be, too. And when you need to be home, you can."

"Thanks for the offer."

"But?" Eric prompted.

"But that's not something I ever considered. Even the idea of it sounds crazy."

"More money for the same job you do now plus autonomy? Gee, man. Wild." Eric laughed. "Just think about it. I don't need an answer tomorrow. The door is always open. I've got some top-secret clearance that makes me think that I'm going to need more than one pilot for the foreseeable future."

"Okay, I'll think about it." It would take some pretty serious life changes for that to happen, but the idea wasn't without merit.

"But not while you're on this mission. Let me know when you're back safe and sound. I'm sure Kentucky will want to know, too."

"I will. Take care, brother." Sean hung up.

AND FOUR DAYS LATER, when his chopper went down over the Colombian jungle, Kentucky Lee was all he could think about.

All the reasons why he had to get back to her, and all the reasons why he should just let things end as they had.

In many cases, the reasons were one and the same.

While Sean was looking up at a canopy of trees, hiding in underbrush from the guerrillas who'd shot him down and praying to God Almighty that the clutch of giant bird-eating spiders nesting near him didn't decide he looked tasty, he wondered what she was doing.

If she missed him.

If she thought of him.

If she understood why he'd had to leave.

When he heard the men hunting him murder tribes-men while questioning them as to his whereabouts, he wished he could hear the sound of her voice.

Even when he considered showing himself to save those innocent lives, he wondered what she'd want him to do. If she wanted him to come home to her a coward for holding his position in the darkness and letting men die to preserve his secret, or if she'd rather he die a hero.

He didn't want to die, but if he had to, he'd rather go out having made the world a better, safer place.

But if he revealed himself, these people still wouldn't be safe. They'd still be under the thumb of this cartel.

He kept thinking about completing his mission.

He kept thinking about going home.

But first he had to find the rest of his team. He wasn't about to leave anyone behind.

These fuckers had already killed other operatives. Sean Dryden was going to wash that blood off their hands with their own. There was no prettier sight, other than Kentucky Lee with the moonlight on her hair.

He moved stealthily away from the tiny hidden village and looked for broken underbrush, twigs and torn leaves. He looked for signs or markers carved into trees, something—anything—that would help him find the rest of his team.

There were predators in the jungle that were almost as dangerous as the men who hunted them. Almost.

As soon as he knew they were going down, his team had jumped. They were several miles away from the drop site. He knew anyone who could make their way there would.

Even with his head in the game, Kentucky was still there in the back of his mind. Still waiting for him in a place that was soft and smelled of home. It burned away the scent of gunpowder and fire in his nose.

He kept moving, kept searching, determined that things wouldn't end this way for him or his team.

Sweat poured down his face, the humidity making

all movement feel like walking through warm water, making every inhalation feel like breathing it, too.

He heard a rustling up ahead, but he couldn't risk calling out.

Then the world went dark.

11

KENTUCKY HADN'T BEEN surprised to find him gone when she awoke. She'd known it was coming. What had surprised her was the note.

Although he'd been gone now for a month and no one had heard a damn thing from him. Not even Eric.

It would be easy to think that he'd exorcised his demons and now he was just done with them and everything from Winchester. It was what it looked like on the outside.

But she knew Sean better than that.

She was worried something had happened to him, felt it in her gut with a sure knowing the same as she'd known her aunt had died before she got home from school the day she passed.

Kentucky was so sure that she'd badgered Eric into using his connections to find out if he'd made it back yet.

Apparently, the mission he'd been called on had been open-ended. It was to continue until they ran out of funding or the mission was accomplished.

Which in Kentucky's mind meant no one had heard from him and he was dead.

It would almost be better if it were that easy, but she knew it wasn't. She knew he was still alive and felt it in her bones. She needed to do something to help him, but she didn't know what.

It didn't help that she'd been sick as a dog for the past week. She could barely keep anything down except pizza and sour gummy worms, and that wasn't exactly the picture of health.

Kentucky had started telling her customers that if they wanted to get their vehicles in, they needed to call in advance instead of just dropping them off. That way she could still get their business but she didn't have to keep the garage open when she felt like shit.

Rachel had come over and brought with her some chicken broth, which so far had been sitting okay.

"Thanks, Rach. You're a gem. Are you sure you want to sit here and eat with me?" she said over the small round table covered in red gingham that sat in her kitchen. "I could be contagious. This flu is a real bastard."

"Honey," Rachel started, "I don't think you have the flu." Rachel pursed her lips.

"Well, what else could it be? Food poisoning? I've had it for a long time."

"Yeah, not that either." Rachel looked at her expectantly.

"What are you...?" Kentucky raised a brow. "Um, no. We were so careful. There is no way I'm pregnant."

"Are you sure? The only way that's one hundred

percent foolproof is to not let him park his car in your garage, if you know what I mean."

"Of cour—" Shiiiiit. The last two times they'd had sex, he hadn't worn a condom. She had been planning to go to the pharmacy for the morning-after pill and she just…hadn't. "Oh my God, Rachel."

"Hey, don't freak out. Everything is fine. No matter what happens, it will all be okay and I'm here for you. Whether that means I go with you to the doctor once—" she nodded meaningfully "—or I'm there with you holding your hand when the baby is born, or if this is just a scare and we'll laugh about it over beers and pool tonight at Eddie's. Okay?" Rachel kept nodding.

"Okay." She inhaled, holding her breath for several seconds before exhaling. Kentucky repeated the act several times before she felt as if her world had come back into focus.

There was a niggling little voice in her head that told her that if she just went to bed and hid herself under the covers, this would all go away and she'd feel fine in a few days.

But it had already been a few days and she felt like shit.

She'd also missed her period.

When the headaches had started, she'd thought it was just her hormones because her period was about to start.

"Here's what we're going to do. We're going to finish the soup. Then we're going to go to the drugstore and we're going to buy a test."

"Two tests," she interrupted.

"Five if it will make you feel better, but you're going to have to drink a lot of water," Rachel ribbed.

"My mind is going a thousand places at once. Some are amazing and beautiful, and others are...not so much. Others are terrifying and I have never felt more alone. I've never missed my mother and my aunt the way I do in this moment right now. I've never been more in need of their guidance."

"I can never take the place of your mom, but you know I'm here for whatever you need. My mother, too. Hey, you know..." She gave her a wicked grin. "If you give my mom a baby to fuss over, maybe she'll stop bothering me."

"You are so not funny. Not in the least." But Kentucky smiled anyway.

"So before you put the cart too far before the horse, before both of us do, let's go get the test."

Kentucky tried not to let her mind run every scenario, but she couldn't help herself. What would she do if she was actually pregnant?

More important, would she tell Sean?

The problem wasn't that she was afraid he wouldn't help her. Or that he'd be angry. He'd do the right thing.

If she ever had the chance to see him again.

She tried to push it out of her head, but it was there in the back of her brain like some chant.

Her world was about to change no matter what the test said.

There was part of her that hoped for both outcomes.

The idea of a baby wasn't as terrifying as she'd initially thought. Especially Sean's baby. Her whole life had been building up to chasing freedom, but she realized that freedom wasn't really what she wanted.

She was pretty free now. She had nothing tying her to Winchester. Not really. Her family had all passed and her business, well, she could move that anywhere.

No, the truth, the real reason she hadn't finished Betty, was that she wanted roots. She wanted a family.

If she was pregnant, she'd get that.

It would be a small family. Tiny, really. Just her and the little life she'd brought into the world. Suddenly, that sounded like a little bit of heaven.

But it was terrifying, too. It would force her to make choices for her child instead of herself. It would cause her whole world to shift.

If she did see Sean, if she was able to tell him, he'd demand to be part of everything even if it wasn't what he wanted.

He'd have the right to an opinion on her life because it would affect his child. They'd be tied together forever.

And if she wasn't pregnant, this realization about home and family would be the loneliest, saddest place she could go inside her own head.

So she guessed it didn't matter what the test said.

Her life had already changed, as had who she was inside.

She'd never been such a twisted-up mess of hope and fear.

Kentucky's thoughts were on a loop as they drove to the store. As they paid for the tests. They seemed to have more weight than just two little paper boxes should in a small plastic bag. As she carried them out of the store, it was like hauling bricks.

Rachel stopped at the grocery store and bought some ice cream. She just seemed to know that Kentucky would need it no matter what the test told them.

She took both tests in rapid succession and placed them on the sink counter to wait.

They were both almost instantly positive.

Kentucky waited, afraid to breathe, afraid to hope, afraid to experience any feeling until she knew unequivocally what the results were.

She waited three minutes. She waited ten minutes.

They were both still positive.

She was pregnant with Sean's child.

The terrified feeling didn't go away and she started crying. Not just watery eyes or a few tears slipping down her cheeks, but big ugly sobs.

Rachel knocked on the door softly. "Kentucky, honey…are you all right?"

"No. Not at all."

Rachel pushed the door open gently and, seeing the positive tests, pulled Kentucky into her arms.

"It's all going to be okay. I promise you." Rachel stroked her hair.

Kentucky let herself be comforted. "What am I going to do?"

"What do you want to do?"

Kentucky dared whisper her secret desire aloud. Dared to fling it out in the universe and own it. "I want to have a family. I want to be a mother."

"Then that's what you'll do, my dearest." Rachel

hugged her tight. "On the plus side, this gives us an edge when it comes to getting information about Sean. We'll be able to talk to his commanding officer and while we won't get any classified information, they'll be able to tell us a little more. Or get a message to him."

"I'm terrified to tell him," Kentucky confessed.

"Why? Do you think he's going to be an asshole?"

"No, I know he won't be. I know he'll do what he thinks is the right thing."

"I understand. You want to be wanted for you, not for the baby you made together."

Kentucky nodded. "And it's more than that. He doesn't want any commitments tying him down and with his job, I don't blame him. I wouldn't want to live that way."

"What do you mean?"

"Never knowing when he's coming back, if he's coming back? Living like this, like we are now, in the shadow of doubt. We don't know if he's alive, dead or just what's going on. But I'd never ask him to give up part of himself."

"You wouldn't have to ask."

"I know." Kentucky shook her head. "Which is why there's this part of me that just doesn't want to tell him."

"That's not fair, honey. I know this is scary, but he deserves to know. Can you imagine how that would feel to him that you didn't trust him enough to share this with him? Or even your baby when she is old enough to ask? You've never been a liar."

"No, I haven't. I wouldn't do that. It's just all of these feelings are so intense."

"If it's okay with you, I'm going to tell Eric so he can try again to get some answers."

"Yeah, I'm going to have to if I want to talk to Sean. Tell him." Kentucky bit her lip. "I hope he's okay."

"I bet he's fine. We'd know if he wasn't."

That was the problem. Kentucky did know. He wasn't fine.

12

SEAN DRYDEN HAD managed to get his team to safety, and for that, he was grateful.

What he wasn't so grateful for was that it had been at his own expense. He knew that as a hero—and all spec ops operatives were supposed to be heroes—he was just supposed to be thankful that his death could serve the greater good.

He was supposed to be willing to lay down his life in the execution of his mission.

But he wasn't. He didn't want to die. He wasn't ready.

Trading his life for that of his team was supposed to be an honor, but he'd admit that he only felt as if he'd gotten screwed.

He was glad they were safe and he wouldn't wish for any of them to be in his place, but his place sucked at the moment.

He'd experienced pain like he'd never imagined before this moment. The horror wasn't just in the pain; it was in the knowledge of the things that this man, this specialist in torture, was doing to his body. The irrevocable damage that made him wonder if he did survive, if he'd even want to.

A spec ops pilot was no good without his hands.

Hell, as a man, he felt as though he had nothing to offer the world. There was no place for him, nothing he could contribute. He'd be a taker, needing a full-time nurse.

Sean looked down at his hands, seeing the mangled mess the guy had made with the hammer. He didn't know how reconstruction could even be possible.

If he made it out of this sweltering shit hole. He didn't know how long he'd been there, but having a better idea of where was more important.

He knew he wasn't far from a secret CIA facility that could get him home; he just had to escape this fuck and navigate the jungle—without using his hands.

A task that seemed nigh on impossible.

He'd lost feeling in his shoulders some time ago, suspended as he was. He hadn't decided if that was a blessing or a curse.

He thought about Kentucky—her smile, the way her hair looked spread out on the pillow behind her with her cheeks flushed after making love. She was so beautiful. He wanted nothing more than to see her face again.

He'd tell her.

He'd tell her that he loved her, tell her that he wanted to be with her. He'd tell her that she was more than just a Band-Aid for his grief and guilt over Lynnie. He needed to tell her that. Needed her to know how much she meant to him—how much she'd always meant to him.

Even though the last day they'd spent together had been something amazing—the very fabric of summer memories—it couldn't be the last one ever. He couldn't live with the idea that the last thought she'd ever have of him was him sneaking out of her apartment in the predawn hours after an amazing night without so much as a real goodbye.

He should've woken her, should've told her then that he'd see her again. That he wanted more than temporary. That would have given her time to think and it would've given him some piece of mind that he'd not hidden from living.

As Kentucky always said, he should have lived a little.

Because now, in these moments that could be his last, he felt as if he hadn't lived at all.

He wasn't going out like that.

So what if his hands were in agony? The pain meant he was still alive. As long as he could feel the pain, as long as he could still suffer, he was still breathing. Still had more living to do.

He scanned the room again and again for some way to free himself, but there were still no good options. He'd have to wait until the man with the hammer came back.

He was supposed to start on Sean's knees next. If he didn't make something happen soon, there would be injuries there was no coming back from.

Even with his hands as wrecked as they were, he could fight through the pain. If he damaged himself further, so be it.

When the man came back, his body launched into action before his mind could make the conscious decision to move. He surrendered to his training and it was as if space and time blurred. He'd wrapped his legs around the man's neck and even though the man stabbed at him with a scalpel, he kept squeezing until he was dead.

He managed to pick up the scalpel with his toes, and in a feat of superhuman strength, he lifted his leg to the rope that tied him and pushed the blade back and forth across the heavy weave until he was free.

Landing on the sawdust-covered floor, he saw that he left a trail of blood behind him.

That wouldn't bode well for his survival in the jungle.

But he had to risk it. He might die in the jungle, but he would for sure die here if he stayed.

So he ran. He ran out into the darkness with blood dripping from his hands, out into the humid foreign jungle, where the apex predators had come out to hunt.

The night birds and other animals made quite the ruckus, with howls and caws and even the occasional roar of a jungle cat after the screams of its prey. Those sounds comforted him because if they were consuming that prey, they weren't stalking him.

Not like the thugs at the compound he'd just fled.

Sirens blared loud and he realized they must have noticed his escape. The Humvees they'd sent out to hunt him roared and echoed in strange directions, momentarily disorienting him.

He looked up at the stars, using the planet Venus to determine his position. He knew if he kept heading south, he'd find that base and, hopefully, an evac.

The darkness was absolute when he moved deep enough that the canopy of trees obscured the night sky, and the method of his navigation.

He closed his eyes and breathed deep, recalling his training. He'd flown in fog with nothing but the altimeter working. His inner compass wouldn't lead him astray.

A cold numbness had started in his feet and was slowly working its way up his leg. He realized he had another wound. He'd cut himself somewhere with the scalpel and he was losing blood faster than he'd anticipated.

His vision started to blur and he stumbled, crashing down to the jungle floor.

WHEN HE AWOKE, he was surprised. Surprised to be awake and alive. His hands were in bandages. So was his leg. But he could still feel all of his limbs—they hurt in ways he hadn't known were possible.

The room he was in was large, sterile and white—a hospital room. The scenery outside of the window was familiar—it was home.

And sitting in the chair by the window, with the warm light of the sun falling around her like a halo, was Kentucky.

She was sleeping, her red cowboy boots propped up on the edge of his bed. That splash of color so bright in a world of white and grays. It made everything so much more real somehow.

He wanted to reach out and touch her, but he couldn't with his hands bound as they were and, he realized, in traction.

Jesus Christ, it was humiliating for her to have seen him this way.

But you're alive, he told himself.

You made it home.

It must've been serious for Kentucky to be at his side. They must've gotten in touch with Eric. Otherwise, how could she be here?

She shifted in her sleep and turned her face toward the sun, which caused her to stir to wakefulness.

The look on her face when she saw his eyes were open told him that he'd been closer to death than he'd ever imagined.

Kentucky's eyes were luminous pools of unshed tears.

She looked at him, gesturing helplessly.

He knew exactly what she wanted—needed. Contact, touch. But she didn't want to hurt him. "Come here, baby." Sean nodded his head. Even that action was a little uncomfortable, but he didn't care. He needed the same thing she did.

She inserted herself in the bed next to him, ducking under his arm and resting her head against his chest while carefully embracing him.

"You're not going to break me. I can't hug you back, so you have to do it double for both of us."

"They thought you were dead," she breathed.

"Takes more than that to kill me."

"Not much more." She tightened her hug incrementally until she was pressed hard against him.

"It probably looks worse than it is." He decided to put on a brave face for her. He wouldn't lie—he was afraid of what had happened to him, what it meant and what his life would be like. But she didn't need that on her shoulders.

"It looks pretty bad. You've been here for two weeks. They were wondering if you were ever going to wake up. I need to get the doctor."

"No, no. Give me just a minute with you." He breathed in the scent of her. "I don't even know how you're here."

"It's not me who is here but you. You're in KU Med. Eric used his connections to get you transferred here from the hospital in South Carolina after they pulled you out of Colombia. You've been under sedation waiting for the swelling in your brain to go down."

"Jesus." He wondered how much more he'd lost than just the time.

Her shoulders quivered and he could feel the heat of her face against his chest. She was crying.

"Hey, Tuck. I'm okay."

"Yeah, but you weren't. And I knew you weren't. I could feel it." She clung more tightly to him. "I thought you were going to die and I…"

He wished he could touch her, soothe her, but his goddamn hands…

"But I didn't. I'm fine and you're here with me."

She pulled back and looked into his eyes. "That really makes it better?"

"Of course it does. I wouldn't have left if I hadn't been recalled. I didn't lie."

The expression on her face softened. "I know you didn't lie, but I also know that what we were doing was going to end eventually. And that's okay. It's not the time to talk about it anyway."

Suddenly, he wanted nothing more than to tell her he wanted to be with her, but that wasn't fair to her. Especially not knowing what his mobility was going to be like, the extent of his injuries.

He believed that you should care for someone through thick and thin, but he wasn't about to hang himself around her neck like an albatross.

But one small part of his confession couldn't hurt, could it? Something to let her know if he made it through this, if she wanted him, he wanted to try having a relationship with her. "Tuck, all I could think about out there was you."

"What do you mean?"

"Let's talk about it after I get out of here, okay?"

"I... I..." The expression on her face looked almost as if some witch had stolen the words right from her lips. She just nodded and leaned back down, her face buried in his neck.

"If only I could touch you, the things I would do to you right now."

"Really? You just woke up and you're thinking about that?"

"I think about that in my sleep. I think about it awake. I think about it every time I'm anywhere near you."

"So if I were to do this, you'd like that?" She pushed her hand beneath the sheet and over his chest.

"Hell yeah." His cock rose to salute her.

At least there was nothing wrong with that.

She pushed the hospital gown up higher until his chest was bare and she lay her head over his heart, dragging her nails lightly up and down his flanks in the most delicious way.

"I just want to hear your heart. It's so strong, beating solid against your chest like you didn't almost die. Like you're not..."

"I told you, I'm fine."

"I couldn't stand it, you know."

"What?"

"If you died. It would kill me, too. I can't lose anyone else."

He didn't say anything. He didn't know what to say.

"I'm not asking for any promises. I know what's between us. You were my friend before we slept together."

"Kentucky..." All the things he'd sworn he wouldn't say welled on his tongue.

"No, it's okay. Just don't die."

He thought about what it was like back in the jungle when he believed he was going to die. He thought about how angry he'd been about it. He'd had a pat answer about it being part of the job and he'd even talked himself into believing it, until it was there on his doorstep.

"That wasn't exactly part of my plan."

"It never is. I know you can't promise you won't. You're not a liar."

Oh, but he was the worst kind of liar. He'd been lying to himself. He was no hero. He'd never been worthy of that mantle she'd pinned on him. He was a coward. He was afraid to die, didn't see any honor in wasting a life.

He thought about his team and the others he'd managed to get to safety. One life for many—even if it was
his. If he'd bailed on them, he'd never have been able
to live with the guilt.

So maybe he wasn't as much of a coward as he
thought himself after all.

"Your heart is beating so fast. What are you thinking
about?"

"Honestly? Dying."

She was silent but continued caressing him.

"I was thinking about all the things I want to do but
haven't. I was thinking about how much I really didn't
want to die, wasn't ready to lay down my life. I was
thinking that I was a coward."

She sat up now. "Don't you ever say that, Sean. Of
course you don't want to die. It's not a sacrifice if you
give up something you don't value. Look, I know maybe
some women like to see heroes as superhuman, but
what makes them heroes is that they're all too human.
Men and women who sacrifice themselves for something greater, for the people they love. I doubt that when
their last moments come, it's ever pretty or it's ever
okay. It's fucking terrible. But they do it anyway. Like
you did."

"How much do you know about what happened?"

"More than I should. Eric has top-secret clearance,
since he's a secret squirrel. So I guess everything that
your CO knows."

"Jesus, Kentucky." He found himself saying that a
lot, like many people in her life.

"Yeah, well." She made a dismissive gesture. "And I stand by what I said."

He wanted to shrug it off, wanted to dismiss her words because he knew that she had always seen him as a hero, but he wouldn't discount her like that. Even if he didn't agree.

"Thank you."

She leaned down and brushed her lips against his, kissing him softly. The press of her lips was gentle but firm. It was achingly tender but so damn hot.

He liked her being in charge just a little bit.

"I think I'm in need of some healing only you can give me."

"Oh, really, flyboy? What if the doctor said no?"

"But I say yes. What do you say, my sweet Kentucky Lee?"

"I say you're a flirty charmer and a scoundrel to boot."

"You like scoundrels."

"Not as much as I like flirty flyboys."

"So how about some tender care?"

"I don't know how tender it will be." She slid her lips over his again.

He'd never thought he'd have the chance to do this again, be with her. Maybe he still wouldn't, but there was a part of him that wanted to tell her how he felt, to not waste any of the time they'd been given.

It could be so fleeting.

But he considered his situation again. He didn't know if he'd ever be anything more than a burden.

So he didn't speak of his feelings but instead tried to show her with his kiss. He couldn't even touch her.

Her hand slipped between them and cupped the length of his shaft before stroking up and swirling over the crown with a deliberate, agonizing, ecstasy-inducing slowness.

"Is this tender?" she teased, her lips hovering just above his so that he could taste the sweet cinnamon of her breath.

"Tender as can be."

She got up and went to the door, locking them in and interruptions out.

Her eyes darkened, all trace of sadness in them gone, leaving only what seemed to be a pure desire. Her hands weren't soft, not like the rest of her. But they were knowledgeable, moving over his engorged flesh with a sensual precision.

It felt so good just to have her touching him. The scent of her hair in his nose, the softness of her breasts, the heaven that he could find with her were all experiences he'd thought he'd never feel again.

The fact that when he'd opened his eyes, she'd been here with no judgment, only her concern for him.

He bucked his hips and thrust up into her hand.

She continued stroking him, increasing the pressure and staccato rhythm of her caress as he let her pleasure him.

"Come for me."

Sean had never had a particular bent for dirty talk, but something about hearing it from Kentucky's sweet mouth made it hot.

He wished he could touch her; the memory of her skin under his fingers seemed as if it was so long ago.

She moved so that she straddled him, and she pulled her thong to the side underneath that tight, sexy denim skirt so that he could enter her.

Kentucky was still wearing those red cowboy boots and damn if that wasn't the sexiest thing he'd ever seen.

His Kentucky, wearing her boots while she took her pleasure.

"You're so goddamn beautiful." He meant to whisper it reverently, like a prayer, but instead it came out harsh and guttural.

She tilted her head back as she rode him, grinding into him with seemingly no reservations about his injuries. He liked that; it made him feel as though maybe this wasn't the end of the world. That he would heal.

That he would be useful.

Kentucky bent down and whispered in his ear, all the while her hips still rolling forward, still pulling him deeper, still riding him. "Give it to me, soldier. It's mine."

"What's yours?"

"My pleasure. Yours." She tensed around him. "This. It's mine."

It was such a strange sensation, allowing her to be in charge. Surrendering to her will. But he found he loved it. He loved seeing her with her head thrown back in pleasure, loved the way she demanded his compliance.

The muscles low in his belly tightened and he tried

to fight the wave of bliss as it surged up within him. He wanted this to last longer; he wanted to engrave every second of it on his memory.

But she was right—it did belong to her.

Everything belonged to her. Even his battered heart.

13

KENTUCKY LEE CREPT out of the hospital room once Sean was asleep and told the nurses that he'd been awake but was now sleeping a natural sleep. She'd been assured that he was on his way to recovery.

She hadn't told him that she was pregnant. How could she?

Well, if she was talking about things she probably shouldn't have done...sex with him all bound up like that had been kind of hot. He'd been completely under her control, and all she'd thought about was how to best bring him pleasure.

But he'd loved it.

He seemed different somehow—she couldn't put her finger on what it was. It was something separate from almost dying, from being tortured. It was... She just didn't know.

Kentucky moved through the halls of the hospital quietly, unsure of where she was going until she got behind the wheel of her car.

She needed Lynnie.

Kentucky drove to the cemetery and walked over to her best friend's headstone. She knew that Lynnie had gone to a better place, that she wasn't hanging around in a box. But it comforted her nonetheless.

She sat down and leaned against the headstone. "Oh, Lynnie. Have I ever stepped in it." She sighed heavily, trailing her fingers across the smooth surface of the stone.

"It's a little bit crazy how much I miss you and how much I need you. But if you were still here, I wouldn't be in this position, I'm sure." She sniffed as the tears welled, hot and acidic, in her eyes and her throat became choked with emotion. "I hope you're not pissed at me. I hope this was all okay. Part of me knows that you'd want us to take care of each other. To be happy." She sniffed again. "But there's another part of me that feels guilty because I always wanted him. I wanted what was yours. I got the fucked-up version of your happily-ever-after."

"I don't think that's true." Eric startled her.

"What are you doing here?"

He held up a bouquet of daisies. "Bringing her some flowers so she knows I'm thinking of her." He laid them down and then sat across from her. "It seems like you need Lynnie right now more than I do. But I'm all that's here. So, do you need to talk?"

The tears she'd been holding back slipped down her cheeks. "It's almost like Lynnie sent you to me."

"Maybe she did."

Kentucky leaned against him, letting his brotherly embrace soothe her. "I don't know what to do."

"With what?"

"The baby. Sean. My life."

"That's actually pretty easy in theory. Well, maybe not easy, but simple."

"Yeah, how's that?" She sniffed.

"You were going to tell him when he wakes up and work it out from there, right?"

"He woke up and I didn't tell him." She was ashamed of that.

"That is a lot to drop on someone first thing," Eric offered.

"I don't want to tell him, Eric."

"Why?" He seemed more curious than incredulous, which she appreciated.

She was grateful that he hadn't gone into a long speech about how Sean deserved to know, deserved to be given a chance. He wanted to know why.

"Because he'll do what he thinks is the right thing."

"That's all any of us can do, sweetheart." He hugged her closer.

"No, he...he'll try to have a relationship with me for the baby."

"What's wrong with that?"

"Not for me. Not because he wants me." It was like digging a knife back into her own heart to admit that out loud.

"How do you know that?"

"Because what happened between us was just supposed to be temporary," she confessed on a ragged exhale.

"What if it's not? Don't sell yourself, or the possibility of a future with Sean short. It's scary as hell, but are you really going to tell me that this is the one time that you're not going to take a chance?"

"I don't know that I can afford to."

"I don't know that you can afford not to. Look, maybe this will help you. Before Sean broke it off with Lynnie, she'd been having some doubts about their future together."

"What?" The revelation was like a slap to the face. "She didn't say anything to me."

"No, and she wouldn't have. She didn't want to put you in an awkward position since you were friends with both of them."

"She told you."

"I'm her brother." He shrugged.

"Did she say why?"

"Different directions. Growing apart. The usual stuff. She said he wasn't the same boy she fell in love with and that just maybe they both had something better on the horizon. Maybe better for Sean is you and this baby. You see him in a way Lynnie never did. You see who he is now. That was hard for her."

"That feels a little sacrilegious."

"What, like my sister was some kind of goddess? I love her. She was an amazing woman, but she was human, too. She wanted a future but it wasn't with Sean. Not really. You're not taking anything from her." Eric pulled back and looked at her. "She's the last person who'd want anyone to make a martyr out of her. She was a whole person—she had her flaws. She wouldn't want you to forget that."

Kentucky didn't know what to do with that knowledge or how to process it. As of now, she knew there were no mulligans, no do-overs. It was just her without a safety net.

"I know I have to tell him."

"I guess you don't have to."

"Rachel says I do."

"Rachel is Rachel. She has very set ideas about how things should be done. I do, too. But I also know that you're the one who has to live with your actions. If you want to turn your back on this guy you're completely in love with because you think it's best, that's on you."

What did she think would happen if she decided not to tell him that she was having his baby? How did she think that would go down?

Actually, she'd just kind of assumed that after their liaison was over, she'd never see him again.

Only he hadn't acted like that at the hospital. He'd seemed so happy to see her. He wanted her.

Of course he wanted you—you were jerking him off while his hands were in traction. What man would say no to that?

"I guess I'm just scared."

"Aren't we all?"

"You're not. Sean's not."

"We all are scared of something. No matter how together someone is, they have that one thing, that one chink in their armor that leaves them vulnerable and afraid. When we risk showing that to someone else…"

he shrugged "…we're giving them the tools to hurt us. That's terrifying."

"When did you get so smart?"

"I don't know. Being a big brother with no parents kind of forced it on me."

She realized that Eric hadn't lost just a sister. She was almost like his child because he'd basically raised her. She couldn't imagine the pain he was in and he'd come to her grave and instead of finding his own comfort, he was giving it to Kentucky, just like a big brother would.

"You were a good caregiver, Eric. You still are."

Eric looked down at his hands, took a deep breath and then looked back at Kentucky. "Thank you for saying that. You know, sometimes I wondered if I'd done things differently, just one thing out of sequence, if that could've changed all of our circumstances. If there was something I could've done… But I know that's not how it works. Logically, anyway." He sighed. "I think maybe you're right, that she did send us here to each other because she knew we both needed it."

"I know that I'm not your sister—" she began.

"Yes, you are. Lynnie always called you the sister of her heart, so you couldn't be anything less to me, too."

The tears choked her again and she took Eric's hand and placed it on her still-flat belly. "Our little group of friends is the only family I have left, but that's not all bad," she rushed to add. "On holidays, I'm not stuck with drunk Aunt Maude or Cousin Sticky Fingers. I get to choose my family. I'd be honored if you'd be Uncle Eric."

"It would be *my* honor."

"And, if you don't mind, if it's a girl, I'd like her middle name to be Lynnette."

"She would've loved that, and so would I."

Kentucky felt as though she could breathe again, as though she had solid ground beneath her feet. She knew she needed to go back to the hospital and tell Sean.

It was now or never.

"Thank you, Eric. For everything."

"Anytime, Kentucky." He hugged her and got up, extending his hand to help her up, as well. "You know if for some reason Sean declines to be a man about his responsibilities, you will never be alone. Rachel and I will always be here for you."

"Yeah, I know." She smiled. "But it was nice to hear again. You guys have been like a touchstone in the eye of the tornado."

"Are you going back to the hospital?"

"Yeah. I guess I just needed a moment to breathe, if that makes sense."

"I had a few of those before I asked Rachel to be with me. I get it." He made a face. "Not that our situation was anything comparable, but for a while I was convinced that if I admitted to Rachel how I felt about her, the universe would conspire to take her away from me. I know it's stupid, but after losing so many people, I couldn't chance losing her, too."

"That's mostly how I feel, but with a few other spices."

"I get it, Kentucky. I really do."

"It's strange, but I thought it would be Rachel who really got me on this, but it's you."

Eric smiled at her. "This is what big brothers are for." Her hugged her again and she did her best not to blubber.

They really had made their own little family—her, Rachel, Eric and Sean.

Eric walked her to her car and she drove the forty-five minutes back to KU Med and made her way up to Sean's room.

He was awake, and a certified nurse's aide was feeding him chocolate pudding.

"Doesn't seem like a bad way to spend your day," she said, holding out her hand for the pudding. "You were asleep when I left."

"That'll teach me to fall asleep."

She smiled at the CNA. "I've got this."

"Are you sure?"

"Yeah."

She waited until the CNA left.

"Are you sure?" Sean repeated.

"Sure, I'm sure. Getting to torture you with chocolate pudding sounds like the best afternoon ever," she ribbed.

"It's pretty undignified."

"Dying is more undignified," she replied, and shoved a bite of pudding in his mouth.

"God, I feel like such a pussy."

"Why?"

"Lying here having you spoon-feed me? It's pathetic."

"Hmm, because all the bones in your hands are broken? Yeah, and you're not on any pain meds? That's not hard and strong at all. Neither was the way you got those injuries, saving your team. Yeah, total bitch up."

"Kentucky."

"What? Honestly, I bet I could get women to pay money to come in here and feed you chocolate pudding."

"Why?"

"Because you're a hero."

He growled.

"No, really. Look at what you did, how you survived. Those people came home because of you."

"But what do I have left?"

He sounded so bitter.

"Everything." She didn't understand why he was saying that. "The doctors said that you're going to recover and with enough physical therapy, you can still fly. Isn't that what you want?"

"Yeah, I can still fly. Not combat missions. I won't be spec ops anymore."

"There's more to you than spec ops, Sean."

"Like what?" He seemed so sad and resigned.

"Like how you're a good friend, a good soldier, a good man." She pursed her lips together. "You'll be a good father."

His head snapped toward her. "What?"

Kentucky felt like a deer in the oncoming lights of a semi—trapped, afraid—but she couldn't go anywhere but forward. "I'm pregnant, Sean."

It was his turn to be the deer.

"Don't worry about it. It's not a thing. I just thought you should know."

14

"It's not a thing? Like this isn't a big deal? How can you even say that? Of course it's a thing."

"I promised in the beginning I wouldn't ask you for anything."

"Jesus Christ, Kentucky." Sean studied her for a long moment and saw the lifted set to her jaw, her defensive posture and even the shadows in her eyes. "You shouldn't have to ask. What kind of asshole do you think I am?"

"It's not that. I didn't want to put any more pressure on you, but I knew I had to tell you…or I wasn't going to."

The hits just kept coming. He didn't know how the thought could possibly occur in her mind that not telling him he was going to be a father was an acceptable thing. Like she'd let him go back to duty and he'd never know they'd made a life together.

It gutted him, made him feel utterly unworthy. Bile and venom rose up inside him until he looked at the fear on her face. He saw her fear scrawled over her features. This wasn't just about him.

She had to be so afraid and she'd probably found out while she was alone with no way to get in touch with him. Then to have to come to the hospital… "It's going to be okay. We'll make it all okay."

"Really? How?" she asked, easing down on the bed next to him.

"We'll get married—"

"No." She shook her head. "A baby isn't a good reason to get married."

"Isn't it? Don't you want a family? What about the benefits I have through the army? What about taking leave when I want to and need to? What about benefits to help you if something happens to me?"

She pressed her hand to her mouth as it seemed she contemplated that very thing, shaking her head. "I can't live that way, Sean."

"What do you mean?"

"I can't be married to you, always waiting for the call."

He knew exactly what call she meant. "Fine, when my tour is up, I won't reenlist."

"You can't do that. That isn't what you want."

"What I want is to provide for you."

"I don't need that from you. I have a pretty stable life. I built that myself." She splayed her hand across her heart. "I have a business that I run. With the morning sickness, I've been taking time off and scheduling things as it suits my health."

"Really? Are you going to be able to get under a Hyundai when you're six months pregnant?"

"No, but I have savings. I'm not struggling. I saved a lot of that insurance money from my parents' estate. I'm fine. We will be fine."

"Then what do you want from me?"

"I want you to do what you want. If you want to be part of this child's life, then be present. But if not…"

"There is no 'if not,' Kentucky. Of course I want to be involved. No, I don't just want to be involved—I want to be a father."

"Good. I'm glad."

"But I want to be part of your life, too. I guess I understand why you'd say no. Right now I'm no good for you. It's not fair to ask you that until I can offer you everything I'm promising for real." He hoped she heard the determination in his voice.

She sighed. "It's not that, Sean. It's who you are."

"Are you saying you don't love me anymore?"

"Never said I did love you." Her tone was gentle, but she was defensive and he understood why.

"Say you don't, Tuck." He wished he could touch her face so he could show her with that caress how he felt about her. He knew he could say he loved her and wanted to be with her, but she wouldn't believe him. She'd already made that clear. So he'd have to take a different tack.

"I don't." She looked away from him for a long moment, then whipped her head around, fire in her eyes. "Oh, you are so lucky that you're in traction, because I would kick your ass. How dare you use that against me?"

He couldn't help the smirk that curved his mouth. "So you do love me."

Sean also couldn't help the bloom of satisfaction in his gut. He was going to win her and this family they'd started.

"Yes, I do love you, Sean. But you're the risk I can't take."

"What does that mean, my wild girl?"

"It means that you're the thing I can't stand to lose, so I'd rather not have you. Especially not because you feel some kind of duty to me."

"I know you won't believe me now, but maybe later on you will. After I've proven myself to you. But, Kentucky, I will prove myself. You were all I thought about, getting back to you, hearing your voice again, touching your face... I do love you."

She gave him a sad smile. "That's even worse. You know everyone who loves me dies."

"Where is all your fire? Where's the 'both feet first' girl who took me to Mossy Rock because she knew what I needed more than I did? You weren't afraid of the future then. Why now?" He searched her face. "Unless it's not you that you don't have faith in but me."

"Don't do that."

"Why not? I want to know what's wrong so I can fix it."

"You can't fix everything, Sean. As much as I wish you could."

"Does it look like I think I can fix everything? Look

at me. I'm in fucking traction and I can't touch you, hold you, comfort you or even kiss you. If I thought I could fix everything, I'd fix that first."

"If you could fix everything, what would you do?"

The question punched him in the gut. "Honestly, I don't know. Everything shitty that's happened has brought us to this point. It's made us who we are. To change any of it would change this moment. I'll let you doubt anything except the part where I'm already in complete and utter love with this child. I wouldn't trade that for anything or anyone."

She nodded slowly. "Okay, I guess I can give you that."

"When are we due?"

"March 10."

"Give me until then to prove that I want you for more than just duty."

"No, it's not about only that, Sean."

"You're telling me that we have no chance of a future together?" Her meaning was a knife in his gut that just kept twisting around, slicing through him.

"That's what I'm saying."

He didn't believe that. He refused to believe that. Sean knew that she loved him, had always loved him. He loved her. These were the ingredients for the happy ending he knew they both deserved.

She just had to see that for herself.

He didn't want to push her away or put more on her than what she could handle. "After talking to the doc, it looks like I'm going to get out of here in about a month. I've got reconstructive surgeries on both hands tomorrow. They're bringing in a whole team of surgeons to fix what's broke."

"Yeah?" she asked softly.

"Yeah and if you can give me one thing, give me this time."

"What do you mean?" She cocked her head to the side.

"Come see me while I'm here, while I'm healing. Don't leave me to do it alone. I want to see you. Don't keep yourself from me."

"Sean..."

"Hey, no strings. I'm not asking you to be anything that we're not already. We started as friends—we should still be friends. Now we're having a baby together. Bring yourself and the baby to me until I can come to you." He met her eyes, hoping she could see the earnest truth in his own. "Please."

The wary expression on her face softened into something else. "You're not going to make this easy, are you?"

"I'd try to make everything easy if you'd give me the chance." But how could she believe him? He'd yet to prove himself to be anything more than anyone else in her life.

"I'll come to see you, but only if you promise not to push. If we can just be Sean and Kentucky like we were before Mossy Rock."

"There's no going back. There's no undoing. We're having a child together—I'm not going to pretend that's not happening. And it's not okay that you'd ask me to." He inclined his head. "But I can say I won't pressure you about anything. I hope that's good enough."

She nodded slowly. "I can do that."

And she did.

After he had the surgery to begin repairing his hands, she came every day. She brought him books and read to him. They discussed things like politics and movies, current events, the weather, and every day, he asked how she was feeling.

He didn't want a generic "Okay" or "I'm fine." He genuinely wanted to know, wanted to be included in every last detail.

As soon as his hands and arms were out of traction, he started physical therapy and every day was a struggle and a fight to use his limbs again, but he was determined. Maybe Kentucky didn't need him to be able to provide for them, but he did. He needed it for himself. He needed that light to come back to her eyes.

He needed her to see him like her hero again. He just wasn't sure how to do it.

One thing he did know was that he wouldn't get there with useless hands. So even when moving them as he went through the range-of-motion therapy exercises was more painful than the original injury, he kept going, pushed through.

After a few weeks, he finally felt he'd made progress when she came to see him and he could touch her face.

She sat in the chair next to him, brought him pancakes and a real fork—still a challenge, but one he welcomed. He reached out and cupped her cheek, stroking the arch with his thumb.

He'd dreamed of that moment for so long in that dark hell. Touching her beautiful face, telling her with his hands how beautiful she was, what she meant to him. Hoping she could feel it and know his truth.

A year ago, Sean never would've imagined this was where his life would lead. To Kentucky Lee. He couldn't let her go now that he'd found her.

He thought about all the things he'd done as a pilot, wondered if he'd ever do them again. Suddenly, they weren't as important as getting Kentucky to believe not only that he was in love with her, but that this was also the life he wanted and they could have it together. That no one was going to take it away from them.

She turned her face into his caress and as much as he wanted to speak the words to her again, he decided to take what she'd offered in this moment and not ask for more. She'd asked him for time, asked him not to pressure her.

He'd promised.

But it had been so long since he'd touched her. It was as if his hands were hungry for her skin—as if they were sentient beings and only the touch of her could nourish them. Hell, just being close to her nourished him.

He wondered if he could ever be that for her.

It was a weird dichotomy that she'd spent her teens loving him and now he was the one hoping for a casual smile or absentminded caress.

He decided to treat this like a military campaign, a mission. He'd scope out her defenses and make a plan to break them down so he could obtain the objective— a forever with her.

She took his hand and held it in her own as though it were a small injured bird, stroking the back of his hand, each of his fingers, tracing over the mangled scar tissue. "You're doing so well. The doctor said you've almost got your full range of motion back. Do you know when you'll go back to active duty?"

"I'm not sure. My tour of duty is over and I could get out."

She seemed to scoff. "Then what would you do?"

"I don't know. Maybe fly commercial airliners. Work for Eric."

"You'd rather hang yourself. You said so yourself."

"There's something here that's more important to me than flying Black Hawks." He looked at her meaningfully.

"You can't do that. It's your calling. You were right when you said that the world needs men like you."

"But my child is kind of more important."

She pursed her lips and looked away but then straightened her spine and met his gaze squarely. "Teaching our child to pursue her dreams is important, too. Would you want her to give up her passion if she didn't have to?"

"Of course not, but this isn't her. It's me. Maybe being spec ops isn't what I want out of life anymore."

"You don't have to choose."

"I'm seriously considering Eric's offer with his company."

"It's the same thing, right?"

"Kind of, but not really. I mean, I'll be going into war zones. I'll be doing mercenary work, which really isn't as romantic as it sounds."

"That doesn't sound romantic at all," Kentucky said.

"It's not, but he needs a pilot."

"If it's the same basic work, why not just stay in the

army?" She cocked her head to the side, her expression quizzical.

"Because I'd have more freedom. I could choose not to take missions and ops. If our son or daughter has something important, like a soccer championship or a recital, theoretically, I can be home. I mean, I'd still have to work, so I know I'd miss some things, but not everything. Not like it would be if I was constantly deployed."

"You've given this a lot of thought?"

"Enough. I haven't decided. I guess it depends on you. I know that Winchester wasn't where you wanted to spend your life. Betty's finished, isn't she? Didn't you always say when she was done you were going to hit the road and never look back on this burg?"

She gave him an indulgent smile. "I guess I did say that."

"What are your plans?" he prompted softly. This was the first time he'd broached the issue. He'd not wanted to rock the boat with her coming to see him, so he'd just let things ride. But it was time to start making plans or at least discussing them.

"First, I want to say thank you for asking."

"What do you mean? What else am I going to do?"

She shrugged. "I see it all the time. Friends who've been roped into situations they didn't want because of custody issues or their partner just wanting to have control."

"Kids aren't supposed to be weapons. It's not like I can't do what I do and be based anywhere. I may not want to move to wherever you had in mind, but you do.

You just got pregnant—you didn't suddenly become a different person."

"Maybe I did in a way. Can I tell you something?"

"Anything."

"I still haven't finished Betty. I realized that she represented freedom to me, which was something I didn't think I had. I thought breaking out of Winchester, Kansas, was what meant freedom to me. But I have enough money to just go, if I really wanted to."

She seemed to be searching for the right words.

"Now it doesn't?"

"No." She shook her head. "See, I've had that freedom all along. I'm completely, utterly unfettered by anything. There's nothing holding me here. Or anywhere. That's the problem. I don't want to be tossed around on uncertain seas. I want roots. I want a family. And I realized I had that, too. With you." Then she rushed to add, "With Rachel, Lynnie and Eric, too. Sometimes family is a choice."

"So you're going to stay here?"

She nodded. "I love my business, and I love the people here. I want our baby to have a network of friends, family—those roots that will hold her grounded and strong but give her wings, too."

"I like that way of looking at things."

"Were you really going to move to wherever I wanted to go? I was seriously considering Vegas. There's a great market there for restored Bettys. I could have a pretty thriving business."

He turned up his nose. "Vegas is dirty, loud and expensive. And hot as hell."

"It's a dry heat." Kentucky grinned.

"So is the sun," he grumbled. "But of course I'd go."

"You've done everything you said you would so far." She nodded. "I wanted to tell you that it means so much to me. Not just because I want my way, but because it makes me feel safe. It makes me feel like I really can do this. We can do this and we don't have to lose each other."

"Why would we have to lose each other?"

"Fighting over things with the baby. Where I'm going to live, the job you're going to have, what brand of car seat to use, who will pay for what..." She shrugged. "Stupid stuff where we forget what we meant to each other."

"That is never going to happen. I promise you, Kentucky." It was a promise he meant to keep, the same as any other that passed his lips. "Maybe we should start hammering out some of those things."

Her hand went down to her belly, and then she laughed. "I'm not even showing yet, but whenever I have something I need to think about, I just seem to use it as a kind of touchstone."

"She won't lead you wrong, I'm sure."

"Do you think it's a girl or a boy?"

"We seem to keep saying *she*, so maybe it'll be a girl."

"Would that disappoint you?" she asked tentatively.

"Of course not. Healthy is all I care about."

"Me, too." She sighed. "If it is a girl, I want her middle name to be Lynnette. Would that be weird for you?" She pressed her lips together. "I mean, naming your child after your ex. That's weird, right?"

"No. She was our best friend. We loved her. We still love her." *But that doesn't take away anything from the way I feel about you,* he wanted to say. "If it's a boy, his middle name should be Lyn, too. New life honoring what's lost." He nodded.

She flung her arms around him then. "Thank you."

Oh Christ, but it felt so good to hold her. To feel her softness pressed up against him in perfect trust. He was starved for her—the feel of her in his arms, the scent of her hair, the softness of her skin.

He could drown in her forever.

"Stay with me," he whispered. When she stiffened and began to pull away, he added, "Just for a little while. Just let me hold you."

She sniffed a giggle. "I've heard that before. I know where that leads."

"Nowhere you don't want it to go." He searched her face. "I've kept all of my other promises. Won't you believe I'll keep this one?"

15

KENTUCKY ALLOWED HIM to lean back on the hospital bed and take her with him.

It felt better than anything had in a long time. It felt better even than the first time he'd touched her. The first time he'd made love to her.

She almost believed that she could lay down her burdens on his shoulders and he'd be her shelter, her home, her forever.

It was what he'd offered.

But she knew he'd offered it only out of duty. The worst part was, she knew he'd talked himself into believing it was actually what he wanted. She was going to save him from that. She didn't want him to wake up ten years from now wondering where the hell his life had gone and wishing he hadn't made this choice. She didn't want him to give up being a pilot, give up what he felt was his purpose in life just because she couldn't handle it.

Lying there, cradled in his arms as if she were some kind of treasure, touched places inside her that she'd known were sore without understanding just how broken, how exposed, how very raw they actually were until he strummed them with his kindness and his devotion.

Thinking that her future could be filled with moments like this one almost lulled her into a sense of complacency. Of letting herself say yes to a future with him.

Until fear reared its ugly head and whispered to her all the ways he could, and would, be taken from her.

Until it reminded her what it would be like, even if he worked with Eric—God, then she'd be waiting to hear about losing them both.

There was a new voice in the back of her mind, though, that reminded her what it meant to love someone. It meant opening yourself to pain, to loss, to suffering. But when had that ever stopped her before?

Why should she let that stop her now?

Why, indeed.

She inhaled a deep breath and exhaled slowly.

The life she'd hardly ever let herself dream about was right in the palm of her hand. All she had to do was close her fingers around it and say, "Yes, this is mine."

But she didn't.

Instead she lay in silence with him, holding his scarred hand.

The rest of his recovery passed quickly and when he was discharged from the hospital, he took a room at a motel.

That felt wrong, but what felt right was wrong, too.

She wanted to offer to take him home with her, but she knew that would only lead to something they'd both regret.

All of this would've been so much easier if he were an asshole. Then she could just hate him and never think about him again.

No, that was a lie. She wouldn't stop thinking about him, but maybe she could stop longing for him. Stop missing the way his lips felt on hers, the warmth of his body next to hers. That utter divinity when their bodies were joined...

He came over a few days after he'd been discharged with Chinese food.

When she saw him walk through the door of her garage, her insides melted into a happy glow. The very sight of him was a balm.

She grinned and waved at him. "Is that for me?"

"Yes, ma'am." His grin morphed into a smirk.

"What's got you making that face?" She arched a brow as she took the bag from him, inhaling the scent of the crab Rangoon and egg-drop soup. Her mouth watered.

"You're going to be so cute in those coveralls once you really start showing."

"I'm going to look like a blue beach ball."

"It'll be the cutest thing I've ever seen in my life."

"Are you going to be here?" At the look on his face, she realized she shouldn't have asked. He'd been the one to keep to her rules. No pressure. Now here she was asking if he was going to stay, which would lead to one of those deeper, emotional conversations that she'd said she wanted to avoid. Why couldn't they just enjoy their Chinese food?

Because, that voice answered her, *that's not how these things work.*

"Actually, I have made a decision." He followed her upstairs to the apartment and set the table. "I thought about what you said, about giving up my dreams. And you're right—I don't want to do that."

"See?" Why did that make her stomach sink?

"But if I did, it would totally be my choice. It's something I would choose with open eyes. Eric's offer means I don't have to. I can have both things I want. Time to be a good father and serve my country, while making much better money. So I'm going to tell him tomorrow and file my paperwork."

"Are you sure this is what you want?"

"One thousand percent."

"Okay."

"There's something else I wanted to talk to you about."

She didn't like the sound of that.

"It's just an idea."

Kentucky sat down and stared at him, mouth pursed. She didn't know why she was already feeling so defensive. He'd been nothing but supportive and encouraging. He actually hadn't tried to push his agenda at all.

"Okay, go ahead."

"I think you—we—should consider buying a house." He studied her face for a long moment before replying again. "Your apartment upstairs is only one bedroom. That's not viable long-term. If we buy a house, we can afford more together than alone. We could give the baby a more stable environment instead of shuffling back and forth to each other's houses. And I really don't need a house to myself if I'm taking ops."

She stared at him, unsure of what to say. His words made sense, but the idea was scary. It was relationship territory, even if he denied that was what he was doing.

"I don't know."

"We'd each have our own rooms. I'm not trying to push anything that way. I can't say I'd like you dating anyone else. In fact, it would kill me, but I'm not going to interfere in your life. I just want to be close to the baby."

"Sean…" What was she doing? This man she loved said that he wanted her, wanted to build a home and a family with her.

Why was she so afraid to say yes? Anything could happen. She knew that. Anything bad. Anything good. Why couldn't she just say yes?

"Just think about it. We have some time."

"What about the garage? I like the security of someone living here."

"We could rent it out. Hire someone to help you and make that part of the salary."

"I don't need help."

"You might. I want you to be able to take as much time as you need to and having someone you trust in the shop will give you that freedom."

"What, no offering to cover all of my bills?" That was the last thing she wanted, but it was as though he had this whole thing all planned out with no thought as to how it made her feel or what she wanted. She knew he thought he was doing the best he could for all of them in the situation but he needed to learn to talk to her about it instead of getting all gung ho as if he were the mission commander and she were the grunt.

"Kentucky, if I thought for one second you'd let me, I'd be all over it. But I know how important your independence is to you."

"I really wish you'd stop being so damn perfect." She sighed.

"You know I'm far from it. I'm fighting my own selfishness every day I see you, Tuck."

She bit her lip. She'd wanted to hear it, wanted to know that he was still just as affected by her as she was by him.

She knew that was just as selfish. "I guess I am, too."

"Will you indulge my selfishness? Just this once?"

She licked her lips. "How?"

"Let me kiss you." The plea in his voice was devastating.

"Just a single kiss?"

"I told you, when I was in that hell, all I thought about was kissing you. Coming back to you. I couldn't stand the idea I'd never touch you again, never feel your lips. I touched your face, just like I'd dreamed about. Now let me kiss you."

"You're kind of a bastard." His words drove daggers into her heart.

Maybe he really had meant everything he'd said to her. That just made it worse.

"I'm a lot of a bastard," he agreed.

She stepped closer to him and put her hands on his shoulders, staring up into his familiar face.

Oh, how she loved him. She was practically brimming

with it. He had new lines around his eyes, a new depth to the darkness, and damn if she didn't find that even more appealing than when he'd been the golden all-American boy next door.

She drank him in, standing there before her with his heart on his sleeve and that one small request on his lips. Kentucky reminded herself of how she'd felt when she didn't know where he was, when she knew he was injured.

She reminded herself how she'd felt when she didn't know if he was going to wake up.

She reminded herself that they'd made this child inside her together.

The reality of him standing there, it wasn't something she'd ever thought she'd have.

"Kiss me, then." The way she lifted her chin made it almost a dare.

His lips descended slowly and hovered over hers, their breath mingling, and for a single moment, they breathed as one.

She swallowed hard, anticipation tightening into desire. "Aren't you going to?" Kentucky whispered.

"I want to remember this." He brushed her lips with his. "I want to remember the arc of descent as your eyes close and you tilt your face up to me. The way the light from the setting sun highlights your hair. The smell of your skin, the taste of your breath." He pulled her closer. "The soft press of your breasts against my chest."

Emotion was like a vise and it squeezed her until she couldn't breathe. "Why did you ever say that you had no pretty words to give me?"

"When did I say that?" His crooked thumb grazed across her cheek.

"At Mossy Rock. Before we had sex. You said I deserved pretty words but you had none."

"I still don't." His breathing had become more ragged, as had hers as the intensity of their intimacy notched each feeling higher.

"Those you just gave me were beautiful."

"It's how I feel, but I guess maybe it is beautiful to feel those things. To share them. But that's not what we're doing here, is it?"

"What do you mean?"

"I'm giving you everything—all I have. All my darkness, my fear, my weakness. I'm confessing it all. And you're giving me a kiss." He pressed his lips to hers softly again. "But it's okay because that's all I asked for. All I know I can have."

"You want me to rip my heart open and spill all my guts on the floor in front of you?"

"No. I just want to kiss you." This time the press of his mouth was hard and almost punishing, but there was something just so erotic about the blatant expression of his need. "I want to kiss you until the last star has burned to nothing."

Dear heaven, he should've been a poet. He knew exactly what he was doing, the way his words affected her. He was a smart man. She broke away, panting. "You said you wouldn't push."

"And I'm not. I'm just kissing you. You said I could. I'm going to kiss you all the ways there is to kiss another person and I'm going to tattoo them into my memory so I don't ever forget. So I can keep each one with me."

What could she do when faced with that?

She could burn.

She could melt.

She could surrender.

Kentucky wrapped her arms around his neck and tilted her face up to meet him. Her lips were swollen from the onslaught, bee-stung and tingling. But she wanted more—no, she needed it. She needed it more than the blood in her veins, the heart in her chest or the air in her lungs.

She clung to him, remembering what he'd said about feeling her softness against him, the contrast of his firm chest, the heat of him burning her through their clothes. He was so strong, so vital—so very much alive.

It was as if all of those possibilities that kept her afraid, that kept her from taking everything that she'd always wanted, began to melt.

So she kissed him back.

She kissed him with all the need, all the passion and all the love that had welled up within her, heavy and earthy and somehow effervescent at the same time.

He tightened his grip on her, enveloping her in all that was him.

But she wasn't ready to step off the ledge.

He broke the kiss and held her against him for a long moment before letting her go. "Our Chinese is getting cold."

16

Stopping was one of the hardest things Sean had ever had to do, but he knew it was what Kentucky wanted and needed. So he broke the kiss that burned his soul and acted as though it hadn't happened.

Acted as though it hadn't mattered.

But surely she knew that it did.

She walked, seeming slightly dazed, to the table.

Good. That meant there was a chance she'd been just as affected as he was.

He didn't understand how to fix whatever this was that was wrong between them. She'd always been the girl who told him to drive faster; she was the one who slid down Mossy Rock in her underwear. She was the one who ate moonshine cherries and dared them all to try them. She was the first one up for an adventure and he was sure that was exactly what life together would be like—an adventure.

"I'll buy a house with you," she said softly as she

spooned out the spicy chicken onto her plate. "But I have a few conditions."

Relief washed through him. He'd thought she'd really fight that and if he had to trade never touching her again to be close to his child, he'd do it. He wouldn't like it, but he'd do it. Of course, she could always still drop that on him.

"What do you need?"

"That we go into this as equals. With your new job, you'll be making a lot more money than I will. I'm really torn between trying to find something that's going to be best for the baby and something I can afford, too."

He saw exactly what she was worried about and wondered what he'd ever done to make her think that he was that kind of asshole. "Do you think that if you let me shoulder the majority of the payment, I'll use it against you?"

She placed her palms flat on the table and breathed. "Maybe not at first. Or maybe you won't even mean to, but—"

"Everything we agree to, we can have legal papers drawn up accordingly." He fought his instincts to take her hand. "There are new houses being built in the Pleasant Grove school district."

"I can't afford that." Her voice was quiet, as if she was ashamed to admit it out loud.

"You can if you let me take care of the down payment."

"Sounds like you already have this all planned out."

"Not all of it. There's room in my plan for what you want. It's why I'm asking you."

"Have you already looked at a house?"

"No. Nothing in depth. I just drove by the new development. I thought we could look at one together when we have time. See if it's something you like."

"I never thought I could live somewhere like that. I mean…"

"Look, before you freak yourself out, living there would be to give our child a good home. It will be our house and I don't give a damn about what the neighbors think."

"How did you know what I was thinking?" She closed the distance between their hands. "I've always been poor white-trash Kentucky Lee. This feels like putting on airs that don't belong to me."

"You've never been any kind of trash, Kentucky. And anyone who told you that was just trying to keep you down. They probably didn't understand that wild innocence you've got."

"Wild innocence? When have I ever been innocent?"

"Sometimes I think you still are in a way. When you take those dares, when you leap both feet first, there's an innocence in that. A sure belief that everything will be okay."

"I guess I'm not so innocent anymore. I can't seem to make this leap," she confessed quietly.

"What if I told you that I knew you would? That it might not be today or even tomorrow but you will? Would that scare you?"

"A little."

He brushed his thumb over hers slowly. "Why?"

"It would mean that my future is already set and no matter what I do, I can't choose."

"You can choose. You can always choose. I'm just confident you're going to choose me."

"Why?"

"Because I love you. Because you love me. Because after all of this, we're family."

"I guess we are family, but there's a ghost between us."

"No—"

"Let me finish. The ghost of who you were and the ghost of who you will be."

"I could say the same about you. About anyone."

She took a bite of her food and she didn't answer him for a long while, until she said, "When is your first op?"

"Not until after the baby is born. I told Eric I needed to be here and he understood. The army gave me a medical discharge, so I'm here until I start working with Eric."

"How can you take DOD contracts on a medical discharge?"

"Mercenary work is different."

"Aren't you going to miss being spec ops? I mean…"

"No. I don't care what anyone thinks about me. I know a lot of those guys get caught up in what it means to be spec ops. They start letting it define who they are."

"Doesn't it?"

"No. Being a pilot was my job. There's more to me than that. Just like you're more than a mechanic."

"Aren't you oversimplifying? Spec ops is a way of life. It's a calling."

She knew him better than he gave her credit for. He wasn't looking for a cookie for his sacrifice, recognition. He just had an end goal that was more important than the rest of it. "That I answered only because of you. When are you going to figure it out, Tuck? It's all about you."

She opened her mouth, seemingly to say something, but then snapped it shut again. Kentucky pushed her food around on her plate.

"I don't know. It doesn't seem real. I'm going to wake up and it's all going to be some dream I had the night before high school Winter Royalty." She stopped playing with her food and looked up at him, her eyes clear pools. "And do you know what's going to wake me up? Eric on our doorstep, ringing the bell with his face a mask of grief and regret. He's going to tell me that just like everyone else I loved, you're dead. Stop trying to make me love you. I already do and it's like a shredder chewing on my insides."

"You loved me then and I didn't die."

"I loved you like a little girl loves the lead singer in a boy band. I loved the idea of you. I loved how pretty you were, how you looked down from on high and saw me. What I feel for you now is earthier, deeper, something real."

"That's good. I'm a bastard to live with. Nothing will take the shine off loving me like seeing my laundry on the floor."

She laughed but sobered quickly. "That's just it. I won't see your laundry on the floor. It's going to be in your own room. I'll stay in mine."

That idea sounded so foreign to him—wrong.

He wanted to tell her that she was just being stubborn. There was no reason for them to be apart. If something happened to him and they still hadn't defined their relationship in a certain way, that wouldn't change how it was going to hurt.

But it wasn't a given something bad would happen. Lots of people did the work he did and nothing happened to them. No one could predict how much time he had on this earth, regardless of what job he had. He could be a librarian and fall off a ladder and die tomorrow.

He wanted to say all of this to her, but he understood why she felt as she did. She needed to feel some semblance of control. He knew that as a teen, strangely enough, she'd found control in rebellion. No one could control her actions but her. But now that she was an adult, it was a little bit different.

"If that's how you want it, but I'm going to tell you what I want. I want to see your face when I wake up in the morning. I want to hold you when we go to bed at night. I want to have more babies with you. When we're old, I want to be surrounded by our grandchildren."

"But what if we don't get old?" It was more than a question; it was a dissection of her heart on her sleeve.

"Maybe we won't, but for me, I'd rather spend the time I do have loving you."

"You don't understand."

"Don't I?" he asked softly. "Don't I just? Maybe I wasn't in love with Lynnie anymore, but I still loved her. I still lost her."

Her shoulders slumped. "I know that. I guess I just

forget sometimes. I'm caught up in my own feelings."
She shrugged. "My own fears."

He just wanted to fix this for her, but he didn't know
how.

He wanted to fix it for himself, too.

There was part of him that couldn't believe this was
real. He was going to be a father. He was going to have
a family with Kentucky.

This was everything he'd never known he wanted.

Thinking of it that way made it sound like less, as if
it were somehow insignificant. But it was more. It was
a dream he hadn't known how to dream.

With Lynnie, he'd just assumed these things were
part of their future. The yard, the dog, two kids and a
quiet, normal life.

The idea of those things had started to strangle him,
a garrote pulling ever tighter around his neck.

With Kentucky, it was a golden future.

For a moment, he wondered if maybe he'd been
wrong. What if she'd started to feel like a life with him
was like that same garrote tightening around her neck?

The very idea that he could make her feel that way
was an anomaly. Perhaps that was what she'd really been
feeling all along, not this strange fear of loss.

He put his fork down, got up and began putting his
food in plastic containers.

"What are you doing?" she asked.

"I'm giving you some space. You asked me for it, but
I haven't given it to you. Not really."

She stopped eating and stared at him. "I don't understand."

"I went into this with an agenda. I thought if I could just get you to see how happy we could be together, you'd change your mind. If I could prove to you that I could be a good partner, you'd move in with me. Not just for the sake of the baby, but for me. Because you love me. I said I wouldn't push, but I did anyway."

"What changed your mind?" she asked, her face carefully neutral.

"I was thinking about how I felt with Lynnie and the future we'd planned together in those last days. The way it felt like a noose around my neck. I'd never want to be that for you. So I'm going to go. I'm going to give you that space I promised."

She didn't say anything.

"I'd still like you to keep me posted about doctor's appointments and other decisions. Maybe you can choose a house that you like and we could look at it soon. But otherwise, I'm not going to bother you."

He didn't wait for her answer, but instead walked out the door without looking behind him.

Because if he looked back, he'd never find the willpower to leave.

So he walked to Eddie's for a beer.

He found himself a nice dark corner and sat alone with his lager and all the things he didn't want to feel.

Sean thought about getting good and drunk but knew that wouldn't help anything. He watched the people in the bar and thought about what their lives must be like. If any of them wished they'd done things differently.

Like Old Man Pike. They called him Old Man as if

that were actually his first name. He'd been a fixture at Eddie's bar since Sean's father was a kid, he was sure.

His wife had left him for his brother and he'd never been the same since. Never held a job since. Never did anything but drink up his Social Security check.

He didn't want himself or Kentucky to end up that way, so bitter that the only thing that could salve their wounds was crawling into the bottom of a bottle.

He'd done everything he had to try to make things easier on them both.

But maybe being with him wouldn't be easier for her. Maybe he was wrong about her and being able to handle the kind of work he did, the kind of life he offered her.

As much as it sucked and as much as he claimed he didn't want to sacrifice himself, he'd do it. Because he wanted her to be happy. He wanted her to follow all of her dreams and catch them in her net, even if it meant not being with him.

Love wasn't selfish. It was kind; it was generous. It wasn't about holding on; it was about letting go.

That revelation slapped him in the face with a wet towel. He'd been trying to hold on much too tightly.

She knew how he felt about her and the baby. Knew what he wanted. If she wanted it, too, she'd come to him.

If she didn't, it would wreck him, but he didn't want her unless she came to him of her own free will. Came to him because she wanted a life with him, the life he'd offered and was capable of giving her.

He knew that she might well not want that. She'd said she couldn't stand the idea of not knowing where he was, of knowing that he was in dangerous situations. That was asking a lot of her, especially with all she'd been through.

He took another drink of his lager, trying to stop his head from spinning with all the reasons she had to say no.

17

KENTUCKY HAD TO finish Betty.

She couldn't explain exactly why, but it was something that had to happen. There wasn't much left to do. She took one more bite of her food before saving it for another meal. She wasn't really hungry anyway.

She hadn't bothered to take off her coveralls before coming inside to eat, so she headed back down to the shop.

All that was left was to attach the chrome fender.

She'd put it off for such a long time. What was she waiting for?

And then she knew. She was waiting to know what she truly wanted to do with her freedom. Part of her had been waiting for her conscious mind to realize what freedom actually meant to her.

It wasn't Betty.

She was ready to let go of that crutch.

As she positioned the fender in place and secured it, she realized she was ready to let go of Betty, too.

It was strangely freeing.

Like shedding twenty pounds off her shoulders.

She looked at Betty, and for a moment, she wished Sean were there to see it. This had been so important to her and she wanted to share it with him.

It occurred to her that if she accepted his offer, this was how things would be. He wouldn't be here when she needed him.

She shook the thought out of her head and continued to survey her work until the garage buzzer rang and she went to see who it was.

Billy Doniphan stood outside with a small box with yellow wrapping, smiling sweetly. She opened the door.

"Hey, pretty lady."

"Hi, Billy. What can I do for you?" She'd just run a diagnostic on his truck, but she was sure that he was trying for more time with her rather than actually needing any kind of service to his truck.

"I brought you a little present for the baby."

"I guess I'd better let you in, then, huh?" She smiled at him and opened the door. "How'd you know I was pregnant?"

"A town like this? Everyone knows." He handed her the small package when he stepped inside.

"Thank you," she said, accepting the gift.

"I hope you don't mind me asking, but it's Dryden's baby, isn't it?"

Kentucky narrowed her eyes.

"I don't mean any disrespect." Billy held up his hands, as if that could ward off her glare.

"I guess everyone in this town knows my business anyway. Yes, it's Sean's." Her right hand went protectively to her stomach.

"Is he doing right by you?"

Billy thought he was going to look out for her. She supposed that was nice, even though it wasn't something she'd asked for or wanted. "Yeah, he's helping as much as I'll let him."

"Remember what I said about other people in the world?" He looked down but seemed to force himself to meet her gaze straight on. "About me."

She nodded.

"I don't care that you're pregnant with another man's child. I'd be a good partner to you. A good father. I know you don't want to hear that right now, but later. When you're alone and you need someone. I hope you think about me."

It rankled her that he automatically assumed Sean wouldn't stand by her. She knew he thought he was saying the right things, but he couldn't have been more wrong.

"Billy, I don't want to be with someone just so I'm not alone."

"You might change your mind after the baby comes. It's hard work raising a child all by yourself."

As if she didn't know that. As if she didn't understand what hard was. She knew what she was getting into. "I won't be by myself. Sean will be a good father."

"Is he going to marry you?" The way he posed the question suggested he already knew the answer and didn't like it.

"It's not 1867, Billy. I don't need to be married for

any other reason but that I'm in love. I have my own business that does okay. I have insurance. I have a roof over my head. I have friends. My life is actually pretty close to perfect." Although that was a lie. It wasn't anywhere near perfect, but with enough work, maybe she could get there. Everything else she'd said was true.

"There's a way things are still done in small towns. You want to move to Kansas City, maybe you'd be okay. But here? It was a stretch for these people to bring their cars to you because you're a woman. Now you're an unmarried single mother."

She knew he was just trying to be helpful, but he was really starting to piss her off. "How does that affect my ability to fix a car?"

"You know it doesn't. But it affects the people who live here."

"Then I guess they can take their cars elsewhere. Into the city, where they don't know anything about the mechanic, who can take them for a ride and charge them twice what the work is worth, and contribute to his sinful ways, too. Me, I'm just going to be a mother. Those other guys? Who knows what they're into, but hey, whatever." She hated how defensive and angry she sounded.

But what right did they have to judge her?

"Kentucky Lee, you know I'm just telling you the truth of it."

She sighed. "I know, Billy." She searched for the right words to say.

"It's not like it would be a hardship for me. I'm not

offering trying to be self-sacrificing. I'd be honored if you'd give me a chance."

Something settled in her chest, heavy but warm. "I'm afraid no one has a chance but Sean. I've loved him since we were kids."

Fear of losing him and all.

"I understand." He nodded slowly.

"I'm sorry, Billy."

"I'm not. I hope you get your happy ending with him. Because the way you feel about him is the way I've always felt about you."

She didn't know what to say. The revelation startled her. She didn't know why, since he'd always been trying to ask her out and she'd always said no. But he kept coming back to the well even though it was always dry.

He didn't wait for a response from her. "Open the present."

She smiled at him and pulled off the slick yellow paper. Inside was the tiniest pair of soft sole tennis-style shoes with teddy bears stitched into the side.

Kentucky hugged him. "These are so cute. I love them. It's the first gift the baby's gotten."

"I'm glad you like 'em. I'm gonna go now."

"Hey…" she began.

"What?"

She wanted to say something meaningful, but she didn't want him to get the wrong idea. So all she said was "Thanks."

"Anytime." Billy left and he didn't look back.

She didn't know why she found that to be so significant, but it was somehow. It was about looking forward to the future. Not being stuck in the past.

And not being afraid.

She'd never let it control her before, so why was she going to start now?

Why would she keep hold of a shadow idea when she could have it for real? Sean said he loved her, and he'd never lied to her before. So why shouldn't she take that at face value?

Why would she turn her back on the life she'd dreamed of just because deep down, she thought she still didn't deserve it?

That was crazy.

This was everything she'd ever wanted.

She texted Sean.

Want to go look at houses tomorrow?

Pleasant Grove? he responded immediately.

Yeah. There's a yellow one with an embossed driveway I'm kind of in love with.

It was the feature of the local realty flyer. All glossy and perfect on the front page. It was the kind of house she'd seen in magazines.

If she saw it in person and she loved it, they were going to buy it and she was going to tell Sean if he still wanted her, he was stuck.

I'll call the real estate agent.

I'll pick you up at ten.

Excitement and anticipation were like dark knots in her stomach. When Sean left, it had seemed as if something had been broken. She could only hope that she could fix it.

Although he wasn't the type to give up without a fight. She had confidence that he meant what he said: he was giving her the space she needed.

It was true—she'd needed that distance, if only for a moment, to realize what she really wanted, why she was afraid of it and how to get it. Pushing her was like pushing a mule. It never got anyone anything until she was damn good and ready.

Even herself, it seemed.

She'd wanted to say yes and had kept trying to push her brain to do what her heart wanted, but it had its own timeline.

Kentucky went back upstairs to her little apartment and looked at the house again. It was everything she was afraid to want, much like a real future with Sean.

What in the world would they do with four bedrooms?

The secret voice in her head that had kept getting louder as the days passed said that they'd fill them with children. The idea of that warmed her from the inside out, a blooming of joy like the petals of a flower unfurling through her veins.

It was just a little bit scary that she could imagine his boots by hers next to the door.

This was real and she was going to grab it with both hands.

She had to talk to Lynnie.

Last time she went, she'd talked to Eric. Almost as though Lynnie had sent him. But this...this was just for her and Lynnie.

How crazy was she that she was going to the cemetery in the middle of the night? Probably certifiable, but it couldn't wait.

She hopped in Betty and drove the few miles to the cemetery and to Lynnie's grave.

As she wandered up the manicured walkway, she wasn't filled with grief and fear. That wasn't to say that she didn't still miss Lynnie with her whole heart—she did. She always would.

But this was more of a goodbye and a request for her blessing.

She sat down cross-legged in front of the headstone. "Hey, Lynnie. Things are a little different since the last time we talked."

Her eyes stung a bit, but it wasn't with the same intensity as before. "I finished Betty. I brought her." She motioned over to the car. "I don't know why I think you can hear me, but there's something inside me that's just really certain you can."

She exhaled.

"Our baby is a girl. I haven't had an ultrasound yet, but I just know. I feel it. Her name is Anna Lynnette. I hope you'll watch over her the same way you watched over all of us when you were here. And I love him, Lynnie. I love him so much that it's terrifying."

Kentucky looked around the cemetery, not really

searching for anything in the landscape but more for the rest of the words within herself.

"Last time I was here I was so afraid it was debilitating. But you and I both know that was no way to live. So now I'm about to jump again and it's possible there's nothing to catch me. I mean, I guess that's always possible." She shrugged. "I think losing Sean would kill me, but if I don't leap with him, I'll lose him anyway, right? Better to take what I can have and drink it all down. Just like anything else in life."

She took a deep breath, inhaling and exhaling for a long moment as a certain peace settled over her.

"I'm here to ask for your blessing. I know that you'd want us to keep living, to be happy. But I wanted to ask you out loud. I wanted to come here and speak the words. Fling them out into the universe."

For Kentucky, it was as if something clicked into place. Something right. Something that told her everything was going to be okay.

She was sure that it was just her imagination, but for the briefest instant, she thought she could smell Lynnie's perfume on the slight rustling breeze.

18

SEAN WASN'T SURE what had changed Kentucky's mind about looking for a house.

He guessed that *changed* wasn't really the word, but what had motivated her to say she was ready to go look.

He wasn't going to assume that since he'd given her space, she was suddenly ready to set up house. He'd just try to be grateful that she'd agree to cohabitation and he'd be able to see his child whenever he wanted.

The roar of the Harley outside signaled that she'd arrived.

He came out of the motel and she took off her helmet. "Hey."

It was a simple greeting, but it seemed to be more than that. Maybe it was the way she smiled. Or maybe it was just that they were going to look at a house to buy together. But something seemed different.

"Did you get in touch with the Realtor?"

"Yeah. I thought maybe you might want to get breakfast at Maudie's first. So I told her to meet us at Pleasant Grove at eleven thirty."

"Sure, that sounds good." She handed him her extra helmet. "You ready?"

He climbed on the back of the bike and they drove the few blocks to Maudie's Diner. It was a great vintage place with bacon and eggs all day. They had a nice selection of old-fashioned ice-cream treats, too. Like egg cream soda.

They sat down across from each other and ordered.

She didn't really say much until their food arrived.

"So, last night," she began.

"We don't have to talk about it. I was pushing and I shouldn't have been."

"No, you weren't. Not really. And maybe I needed to be pushed." She pinched her fingers together. "Just a little bit."

"Well, I feel like a dick. I decided in the hospital that I was going to make this plan to get my way and execute it. I really wasn't thinking about what you wanted and needed. I'd just decided that I knew best and that's how things were going to be."

"Of course you did. A man doesn't do the things you've done without being decisive. Without seeing a situation and distilling it to problems and solutions and making a plan for those solutions and following through. I understand that about you."

She sipped her water.

"Well, I'm glad. So, I'm sorry." He was only kind of sorry. He was sorry that he still wanted to try to get his way and sorry that she didn't see the same solution as he did.

"I went to see Lynnie."

"And?" He took a bite of his bacon. It tasted like sawdust in his mouth, but he decided that was probably just the ashes of all the feelings he wished he could hide from.

"And I said goodbye to her in a way, I think. It was the craziest thing, but I could swear that just for a moment I could smell her perfume."

Something bittersweet twisted in him. "Maybe you did." He didn't have to wonder what Lynnie would think of them now. She'd wish them the best; she'd want them to be happy. If she'd found some way to tell Kentucky that, he'd say she was pretty lucky. If he could talk to Lynnie one last time, he didn't even know what he'd say.

He didn't have anything unfinished with her and he supposed that was a blessing. When they'd said goodbye that night, he hadn't known it was forever. But he'd told her he loved her, and she'd said she loved him, but it was platonic. It was friendship. They hadn't had any loose ends.

"Maybe." She nodded. "I wanted to tell you, I finished Betty."

"That's wonderful. What are you going to do with her?" Was she trying to tell him something?

"I've decided to sell her."

"Why would you do that?" His stomach tensed with unease.

"Because she's done. Much like what I thought she meant to me. Remember what I told you about her?"

"That she symbolized freedom?"

"Yeah. She was everything I thought I wanted, but

not. So I'm going to sell her. Maybe she can be someone else's dream."

"That's heavy. Are you sure you don't want to wait until after the baby is born to make that decision?"

Her eyes narrowed. "Oh, you think I'm overemotional because I'm pregnant?"

He wasn't going to touch that with a ten-foot pole. He could only dig the hole she was about to throw him in deeper. "No, that has nothing do with it. At least, not like you think. You're in a high-stress situation with a lot of changes. Why add to those changes?"

She smiled then. It was a genuine expression and not the baring of teeth that he might have expected from another woman. "Because these are all changes I want. Life isn't just happening to me, Sean. I'm choosing what I want, where I'm going." She put her hand down over where the baby grew inside her. "Where we're going."

"If you're sure."

"You sound more attached to Betty than I am." She laughed.

"Maybe I am a little attached to her. She's been part of your life for so long. I remember when you bought her from the junkyard. I was there when she was born, so to speak."

"I think I should take you for a ride in her before I sell her."

"Maybe I'll buy her." So he could give her back to Kentucky if she changed her mind.

"Maybe I'll let you." She nodded and reached from her own plate to his and stole a piece of his bacon.

"I think this is where I draw the line. No one said I'd share my bacon."

"You'd deny a pregnant woman your bacon?"

"I might." That was a total lie.

"This makes me question all of my life choices. How can I be having a baby with a man who won't give me his bacon?" she joked.

"How can I be having a baby with a woman who wouldn't hesitate to steal my bacon?" he tossed back.

He liked this.

It was all old but new, too. This was them, who they were as friends, before all of this. Before sex, before babies. This was just Kentucky and Sean together. It was how he wanted to spend the rest of his life.

He'd give her all of his fucking bacon if she'd have him. He pushed the plate over to her. "Fine. My daughter needs all the bacon she can get."

Kentucky beamed. "I think it's a girl, too."

"Really? Why?"

"I don't know. It just feels right." She watched him for a moment. "Yeah, I know it's hippie-dippy bullshit, talking about feelings and such. But nonetheless."

"I believe you. When my mother was alive, she liked to talk about how she knew that I was boy." He fidgeted with his fork. "Do you have any other ideas for names if it's a girl?"

"No, not really." She cocked her head to the side. "But you do, don't you?"

"Yeah. I'd like to name her Anna, after my mother. Anna Lynnette."

"Yes. I knew that's what you'd want."

"Really?" He didn't know why he was startled, but he was.

"Yeah." She smiled. "Anna Lynnette Dryden. It's a lovely name."

Gratitude rushed through him, as well as a swell of other emotions that he was having a hard time putting a name to.

"It's a perfect name," he agreed.

"Are you sure about this house thing? Because I'm pretty sure this house is going to be the one. I think we need a code."

"Like what?" He grinned. If she wanted the house, he'd make sure she got the fucking house. He didn't much care where they lived. Four walls were the same everywhere. He just wanted to make sure those four walls were in a good school district.

"Like if we want the Realtor to go away, if we want to talk privately, if you think the house isn't the one we should get..."

"I think that if you want the house, we'll make an offer. I got preapproved through Veterans Affairs for a home loan that will cover absolutely any house in that neighborhood."

She put her fork down. "Are you serious?"

"Of course I'm serious. You know, that whole preparedness thing. I don't want to go look and fall in love with something we can't have."

Silence reigned between them for a long time and it made him think about how true a statement that was. For the longest time, she'd been in love with him and thought she couldn't have him. Now the shoe was on the other foot, so to speak. He could think of nothing but having a life with her and it seemed to be the farthest thing from her mind.

It was funny how the world turned and what was topsy became turvy.

"Now we won't, thanks to you," she finally said.

"I was worried you might be irritated I got approved without you on the loan, but Kansas is an equal-share state anyway." He shrugged.

"You were right to do it. I don't need any more stress at the moment. I'm okay with you taking care of those things for now, but we should talk about how we're going to pay our bills if you're out on an op."

"There's a lot to think about with all of this adulting." He grinned.

"Yeah, and it's exhausting. I think ice-cream sodas are just the thing for that."

"Definitely," he agreed.

When their sodas came, she began spooning the ice cream into her mouth with such a look of pure lust on her face that his cock was instantly hard. The way she swirled her tongue around the spoon made him remember what it was like to have that sweet mouth on his dick and that look of pleasure on her face as he watched her take him deep.

All he could think about was wanting to touch her. He felt like an ass because she was a pregnant woman enjoying her ice cream and he wanted to give her a treat of a much different kind.

She paused in her licking. "What?" Then she blushed, seeming to realize the effect she had on him. "It's good."

"I can see that," he said.

She took another bite, devouring the ice cream with absolute abandon, unmindful of his eyes on her. That added another layer of sex appeal. Until the last bite, when she met his gaze across the table and gave the spoon a final swipe with her tongue.

"You're evil."

"I know." She grinned but then looked thoughtful. "I guess it's only evil if I don't plan on the follow-through?"

"Do you plan on the follow-through?" They hadn't talked about this part of the relationship. If they would still sleep together. They hadn't defined anything and he didn't know where he stood, what was expected of him. He didn't like that part. He didn't know how to keep that light in her eyes if he didn't know her expectations.

"I guess you'll see." She winked at him.

Something had definitely changed between them. He didn't know what, but he was sure he liked it. He decided to let her set the pace. She'd tell him when she was ready.

After they'd eaten and were heading back to the bike, he said, "Thank you for doing this with me."

She looked at him for a long moment. "I wouldn't want to do it with anyone else."

19

Kentucky didn't know why she was nervous.

She guessed because this was a big commitment, not just the house, but Sean. This was her future.

Her daughter's future.

His future, too.

They met the Realtor at the stone sign signifying they'd entered the Pleasant Grove neighborhood. She was driving a dark full-size SUV and led them to the only yellow house in the neighborhood. It was at the end of a cul-de-sac, on a slight hill, and Kentucky imagined what it would be like coming home to this house.

Probably everything she let herself dream it would be and more.

There was that little-girl part of her who'd never had a house of her own, aside from the apartment above her garage, that just wanted to take it, inside unseen.

She reached for Sean's hand and his strong fingers closed around hers.

Together. They were doing this together.

The Realtor stepped out of the SUV. She was a blonde middle-aged woman with chubby cheeks and a pleasant demeanor.

"Is this your first home?" she asked.

"Yes," Sean answered for them.

"And you mentioned on the phone that you're all set to go on the loan?"

"Yes."

"Great." She smiled wider. "This house is really a gem. It's brand-new. It was originally intended for the developer of Pleasant Grove and his family, but they ended up buying in Kansas City. Their daughter is attending a private school there."

Kentucky nodded.

"If you two wouldn't mind taking your shoes off… It's a bit of a muddy day." She nodded at them.

Sean took off his boots and Kentucky took off hers as they stepped inside.

Just as she'd imagined, their boots were side by side. She almost started crying, until Sean took her hand again and squeezed.

"You want it without even seeing it, don't you?" he whispered into her ear.

She whispered back, "Our boots look just like I thought they would, lined up together."

He pulled back from her to look at her face. Seeming to be searching for the answer to some unspoken question.

The Realtor kept moving through the house. She was in the kitchen now. "And we have granite countertops—"

Kentucky grabbed his hand and dragged him into the kitchen.

"Do you have a large family? This six-burner gas stove is fabulous for preparing large meals."

"No," she answered. "Just us and the baby on the way."

The Realtor smiled. "There's plenty of room to expand, too, if that interests you. With four bedrooms and a full finished basement, it's very roomy."

Kentucky wandered through the house, leaving Sean to talk with the Realtor and let her show him what she wished them to see. She wanted to visualize; moving from room to room, she imagined their life there.

Eventually, Sean joined her.

"Do you want it?"

"Yes. Oh, yes."

"I'll tell her to start the paperwork."

"Can you tell her to give us a little while alone? I mean, we're making an offer. Surely we could have a few minutes to talk?" Excitement surged.

"Yeah, of course." He exited through the double doors of the master suite and returned a short time later. "She's thrilled. We have an hour."

She pursed her lips together and she suddenly found that all the things she'd wanted to say had died on her tongue. Kentucky couldn't get her mouth open. Looking up into his eyes, so open, so familiar, the embodiment of her forever, she didn't actually know where to start anymore.

"What did you want to tell me?" he prompted.

She looked at his hands, his beautiful, scarred hands. She loved the feel of them on her own, on her skin. She loved looking at them. Every imperfection, every flaw had become somehow dear to her.

"That I love you," she blurted.

"I love you." His expression was pained.

She knew he thought she was going to say something else about why they shouldn't be together or about what this meant between them, but she wasn't. She was going to make him an offer.

"I was going to bring you here and say yes to your offer, but I've decided that's not good enough."

"What do you want from me?" he said, sounding exhausted, almost resigned.

"I don't just want to live here with you or try this relationship thing. I want everything. If we're going to jump, we might as well climb to the tallest peak. It'll be a better ride on the way down."

"What are you saying, Tuck?" He closed the distance between them, his hands on her shoulders.

"I'm saying that one of us should be on one knee right now. Maybe both of us." She sank down to her knees and he followed suit. "I'm saying that I want to spend the rest of my life with you. I love you and I'm ready to jump with both feet, like you said."

The silence stretched on and on and for a moment, she wondered if all of her recalcitrance had changed his mind. If maybe he'd listened to all the reasons she'd given for why they couldn't be together and had taken them to heart.

Then he smiled and it was like turning on the light after hours of darkness.

"Then I guess there's just one thing to say, my wild Kentucky Lee."

"What's that?"

"That you're going to marry me and live happily ever after."

"Maybe one more thing after that." She put her arms around him.

"Oh, yeah? What could be better than that?"

"That you're going to make love to me here in our new bedroom. We've got an hour."

"I like how your mind works, Mrs. Dryden." He kissed her soundly and all the feelings she'd been holding back exploded in a tidal wave.

This was what it meant to drink down everything that life had to offer. This was what it meant to her to be alive. It wasn't cruising down a country road on her Harley at a hundred miles an hour; it wasn't sliding down Mossy Rock into a freezing Sutter's Pond; it wasn't even eating her own weight in moonshine cherries.

It was loving and being loved.

Not just by Sean. It was believing that she was worthy of that love. It was loving herself enough to take this chance and believing that she deserved to be happy. That she was good enough.

She pushed her hands up under his T-shirt, loving the way his skin felt under her fingers. Loving that no woman but her was ever going to touch him this way again. She loved the wide expanse of his strong chest, the muscled curve of his shoulders, the intensity in his eyes when he looked at her.

He allowed her to peel the shirt off. "Is this the follow-through?" he asked, referencing their earlier conversation at Maudie's Diner.

"Yeah. You like it?"

"I more than like it. Come here." He pulled her shirt off over her head.

Her first instinct was to hide from him. Her body was changing; her previously flat stomach now was just a little round.

He pressed his scarred hands over the small protrusion and looked at her with such an expression on his face that she felt like the most beautiful woman in the world. His hands moved up and removed her bra, cupping her breasts and kneading them gently.

It was a good thing he was being careful with her. Her breasts were oh-so sensitive, her peaked nipples sending jolts of sensation straight to her clit.

She wanted him inside her right now.

But she wanted to show him how much she wanted this; she wanted to give him the follow-through she'd teased him with.

She unbuttoned his jeans and pushed them down his hips, his swollen cock springing free for her attention. He'd gone commando.

The sight of it, so hard and engorged for her attention, drew her. She shoved him down onto his back and leaned down over his cock and wrapped her mouth around the crown.

He groaned, the sound deep and guttural. She felt as though she was the one in control, the one with all the power. She loved it when he was a slave to the sensation. She loved his hips bucking up to push himself deeper into her mouth, the way he watched her when she closed her palm around his shaft.

She especially loved the way he felt challenged to

outdo her when she pleasured him like this. Kentucky knew any level of bliss that she could take him to, he'd strive to push her beyond when it was his turn.

He was a competitive kind of guy and she loved it.

She raked her nails lightly down over his obliques and his body tensed, tightening and flexing, his cock jerking in response to her stimulation.

"It's been too long, Tuck. Don't deny me."

"What do you want? Tell me," she commanded.

"I want to taste you while you taste me."

"That's wicked. Aren't you the least bit ashamed?" Kentucky grinned and stroked him.

"Not a single bit." He pulled her up.

She allowed it and helped him strip off the rest of her clothes.

"I want to remember this moment after we're moved in and this is our bedroom. I want to be able to look at this place and remember that's where it happened. Where we agreed to love each other forever and then drove each other wild. So we never lose that wildness in our marriage, and we never lose it in ourselves."

"Again with the pretty words. You have more of those than you think."

"Only when I'm with you."

He guided her up so that her knees were braced against either shoulder and his hot tongue thrust up against her cleft while she fellated him.

A lifetime of sex with this man would never be a bad thing.

He moved his tongue in time with hers. When she increased the speed and pressure, so did he. He was singularly focused on bringing her to climax, which was hot as hell. She worked his cock ever more diligently, tasting him and the evidence of his desire on her tongue.

Bliss built inside her with every tandem stroke of their tongues.

It had been much too long and she wasn't ready for it to be over yet, but his hands anchored around her hips and dragged her down to his mouth so she couldn't flee the sensation and electric ecstasy bloomed and she shuddered against his lips as he continued to lick and kiss her.

When he released her, she was a boneless mess and he loomed above her. "I hope you're not done, because I'm not."

She hooked her legs around his hips and he pushed into her with no preamble—it wasn't needed. She was so slick and wanting. Her eyes were heavy, but he wouldn't let her escape the intensity between them.

"Open your eyes. I want to see you."

"Mmm," she moaned. "You can see me."

"No, I can see your body. I want to see you. That's only in your eyes, Tuck."

She opened her eyes slowly, dragging her eyelids up, and when she looked into his eyes, she knew what he meant. This joining of bodies was hot; there was an earthy physicality to their pleasure.

But staring into his eyes while they made love, well, that was when it became making love.

Desire surged inside her again and she drew him deeper, kept squeezing him with her inner walls.

She liked watching the play of expressions on his face as he fought his orgasm. She always thought he approached lovemaking the same as he would a kind of op. He had a plan—he evaluated weaknesses and then exploited them until he got the desired effect.

Now she was doing it to him.

And she'd gain his surrender.

Kentucky arched up to meet him, his thrusts hitting her in that place deep inside that caused sensation to spiral outward through her whole body so that she felt it in the tips of her fingers.

She hoped that never changed.

Her entire body quivered in response to the stimulation and he did it again and again until she thought she was going to orgasm yet again.

She wasn't about to be outdone.

Kentucky raked her nails down his back, giving him that edge that he enjoyed, and he tensed, causing him to press into her hard and deep.

She cried out.

So he did it again.

"Surrender to me, Sean."

"I already have," he growled in her ear.

Then he kissed her. His mouth, tasting of her, slanted over her lips and she shared their mutual pleasure.

Despite her good intentions, it sent her over the edge. He followed suit and spilled into her body, hips jerking hard as the aftershocks of their lovemaking consumed them.

"I fucking love you," he said when he collapsed next to her.

She loved the way he said it. As if he was in awe of it somehow, as if it was a kind of magic. Who knew—maybe it was.

"I fucking love you, too." She laughed, breathless.

"Is this everything you wanted?"

"And then some."

His fingers twined with hers. "Me, too."

As they lay together, catching their breath and basking in the sunrise-like sensation of the afterglow, it occurred to Kentucky that she'd gotten everything she ever wanted.

Everything she'd dreamed about in the dark and secret places she'd been afraid to show to anyone else and sometimes even herself.

She'd had a few dark moments where she thought she'd lost, where she thought she'd been beaten, but she'd never surrendered.

Neither had Sean.

She knew they'd be stronger together, and as they faced the uncertainty of life hand in hand, that would be the thing that defined them: no surrender.

Kentucky wouldn't have it any other way.

Epilogue

SEAN DRYDEN HAD been gone for two weeks.

It seemed like the longest two weeks of his life. Every second he spent away from his new family was like a year. He wondered what new things Anna had learned while he was gone. He wondered if their home would still seem like the haven it had been before he left.

He pulled up to the front door of the yellow house and the porch lamp was a beacon lighting his way home.

When he stepped outside, the last vestiges of winter were fading and he inhaled the first scents of the coming spring. Of Kansas. Of home.

As he opened the front door to the new house in the Pleasant Grove development, he was hit with the clean, homey smell of vanilla, baby wash and chocolate chip cookies.

He wandered into the kitchen, where a plate of cookies sat with a folded piece of paper with his name on it. *Missed you, flyboy. Come up to bed after your cookies.*

Kentucky'd made these for him after he'd texted to tell her he'd be home the next day.

He popped one into his mouth and it was homemade heaven.

The house was mostly clean, he noticed. Even the clutter of various things required for a baby was organized. The downstairs changing table was stocked and neat, and all of Anna's toys were in the small tote, as were her pacifiers.

Sean could only imagine the work it had taken to keep everything so perfect. He wondered when Kentucky slept.

He considered just sleeping on the couch to let her rest, but he ate another cookie and held the note up to read it again.

She wanted him to come to bed. Told him to, even. She knew he wouldn't want to wake her, since she got so little sleep as it was.

He got a glass and the milk out of the fridge and poured himself some to dip a few more cookies in. He'd been eating nothing but dehydrated rations on this mission. They were easiest to transport to the jungle. So he appreciated the texture, the scent, the subtleties of the cookies in a way he hadn't thought possible.

It made him think about her hands in the dough. Made him wonder what she'd been thinking about while she made them. If she'd done it while Anna was sleeping or if she'd been "helping" somehow. Most likely just gurgling in the bassinet. Before he knew it, he'd eaten the whole plate.

They were damn good. A few extra days in the gym would be totally worth it. Not tomorrow, though. Tomorrow was all about Kentucky and Anna. He wanted to remind himself why he did this job and to be actively grateful for this amazing life.

He went to go put his plate in the sink and he saw that there were a few bottles that needed to be washed.

Sean unloaded the dishwasher and inspected each item to make sure it was clean before he put it away. Then he loaded the dirty dishes from his cookies and the bottles and ran another load. He wiped down the counters and even prepped a bottle for when Anna woke up in—he checked his watch—probably an hour.

He walked up the stairs slowly to their bedroom and tried to be quiet as he opened the door and peeled off his clothes, watching Kentucky as he did so, drinking in the sight of her. She was beautiful, lying there in their bed with her hair spread out behind her like a fan, the bare pale skin of one shoulder exposed to his view.

He liked the silhouette of her curves against the blanket and couldn't wait until he could touch her again, really touch her. Make love to her. But for now, he was content to hold her close. Sean slid in bed next to the woman who would be his wife and pulled her close carefully. She stirred, sleepy and warm, scooting back against him.

The nape of her neck smelled like cookies. He pressed a kiss to that tender place, inhaling the sweet cookie scent.

And Kentucky, well…she felt like home. Being close to her, having her in his arms like this, it was home; it was family. It was everything.

He loved this house, this home they'd built together, but it would be nothing without her.

"Missed you so much," she murmured.

"I missed you more," he whispered into her ear.

Her fingers laced with his. "Nuh-uh."

"I missed you so much I did the dishes," he teased.

"Mmm. 'Kay. You win." She squirmed against him. "Did you think about me?"

"Every night." More than that, but he knew what she was asking. If he still found her desirable. If he still wanted her. His cock was hard for her right now, but he was happy just being close to her.

"It's been four weeks." She moved her hand to slide between them and cup him.

Her touch was sweet torture. "It has, but the doc said six to eight."

"I'm dying, Sean. For real."

"Baby, give your body time to heal. I'm not going anywhere. You're still beautiful and sexy as hell."

She started moving her hand over his cock, determined to get her way. He allowed the caress, because if she wanted to pleasure him, who was he to argue?

Maybe it wasn't yet time for sex with penetration, but he could damn sure give her some attention with his mouth. He'd longed for the taste of her more than her cookies.

His hips bucked up into her ministrations and she laughed, turning over and sliding down his body, pausing to press her mouth over each of his very defined ab muscles—which wouldn't stay that way if she kept making him cookies—on her way to his cock.

Then Anna's small cries echoed into their room.

Kentucky leaned down and pressed her forehead to his stomach in a kind of surrender with a sigh.

She flopped over onto her back. "Duty calls." Kentucky began to get up.

Sean pinned her beneath him and he kissed her lips hard. "Ah, but, my love, the other sweet girl who has my heart calls. It's my turn and my pleasure to answer."

Kentucky laughed. "Yeah, I guess she gets dibs."

"Especially since that means you get to stay in bed and go back to sleep."

"Are you sure? You must've pushed hard to get home this early," she said even as she snuggled under the covers.

"I can sleep when she's a teenager and hates me." He pressed the blanket in around her.

"Unlikely. When she's a teenager and hates you, she'll be dating inappropriate boys to piss you off. So you'll be sitting outside cleaning your Beretta or something."

He laughed. "No, I won't. We'll give her the tools to make good choices even if she does hate me for a year or two."

"I'm so happy it's a little gross," she confessed.

"Me, too. I never thought a life like this would be a slice of heaven, but it is. When I think about all the ways it could've gone wrong, all the chances we had to screw it up…" He shook his head.

"I can finally say that I got something right." She rolled over and untucked herself so she could reach out and cup his cheek. "I love you, Sean."

"You get a lot of things right." He kissed her again.

"I love you." Sean pulled the covers back up over her. "Now get some rest. I know you're exhausted."

He slipped into his boxers and padded to Anna's room. It was a happy yellow with pink flowers and cartoon-character cars on the wall.

She fussed and wiggled her hands and feet, moving all of her limbs faster when she saw him.

Sean reached into the crib and picked her up, the weight of her precious and sweet. He held her up to his shoulder and she turned her face into his neck, still fussing softly.

"Oh, how I missed you, my princess." He stroked her back through the pink terry cloth onesie.

He carried her back downstairs to the kitchen and prepared the bottle. Sean settled into the recliner with his daughter in his arms and thought again, yeah. His life was kind of perfect.

* * * * *

#903 COWBOY UNTAMED
Thunder Mountain Brotherhood
by Vicki Lewis Thompson
Potter Sapphire Ferguson has been burned too many times.
No more relationships with artists! But sculptor Grady Magee
ignites her passion—and might just change her mind—with his
cowboy soul.

#904 HER SEAL PROTECTOR
Uniformly Hot!
by Jillian Burns
When hardened Navy SEAL Clay Bellamy agrees to act as her
bodyguard, quiet executive banker Gabby Diaz is determined to
take more chances...especially given how hot Clay makes her
feel.

#905 WILD FOR YOU
Made in Montana
by Debbi Rawlins
Spencer Hunt, a rancher living outside Blackfoot Falls, Montana,
just wants to be left in peace. But filmmaker Erin Murphy wants
to shoot on his land—and she won't leave him alone!

#906 TRIPLE SCORE
The Art of Seduction
by Regina Kyle
When good-girl ballerina Noelle Nelson meets bad-boy
shortstop Jace Monroe, not even the injuries that landed them
both in rehab can stop their sizzling attraction. But is this an
illicit affair or something deeper?

———

REQUEST YOUR FREE BOOKS!
2 FREE NOVELS PLUS 2 FREE GIFTS!

HARLEQUIN®

Blaze

red-hot reads!

"Lady, you and I generate a lot of heat. You can head home to catch up on paperwork, but that's not going to change anything."

"Maybe not." She shoved her hands into her pockets and clutched her keys as a reminder that she was leaving. Just because he thought her surrender was inevitable didn't mean he was right. But she could feel that heat he was talking about melting her resistance. "I need to go." She started to turn away.

"Hang on for a second." He lightly touched her arm.

The contact sent fire through her veins. "What for?" She turned back to him and saw the intent before he spoke the words.

"A kiss."

"No, that would be—"

"Only fair. I've been imagining kissing you ever since I drove away three weeks ago. If you don't want to take it beyond that point, I'll abide by that decision." He smiled. "What's one little kiss?"

A mistake. "I guess that would be okay."

"Not a very romantic answer." He drew her into his arms and lowered his head. "But good enough."

The velvet caress of his mouth was every bit as spectacular as she'd imagined. If she stuck to her guns, this would never happen again, so it seemed criminal to waste a single second of kissing Grady Magee. She hugged him close as he worked his magic. She'd figured the man could kiss, but she hadn't known the half of it. He started slow, tormenting her with gentle touches that made her ache for more.

When he finally settled in, she opened to him greedily, desperately wanting the stroke of his tongue. Kissing him was exactly what she'd been trying to avoid, but when he cupped her bottom and drew her against the hard ridge of his cock, she forgot why she'd been so reluctant.

Wouldn't a woman have to be crazy to reject this man? Wrapped in his strong arms and teased with his hot kisses, she craved the pleasure he promised.

Taking his mouth from hers, he continued to knead her bottom with his strong fingers. "Still think we should nip this thing in the bud?"

Don't miss COWBOY UNTAMED
by Vicki Lewis Thompson, available in August 2016
wherever Harlequin® Blaze® books and ebooks are sold.

www.Harlequin.com

Reading Has Its Rewards

Earn **FREE BOOKS!**

Register at **Harlequin My Rewards** and submit your Harlequin purchases from wherever you shop to earn points for free books and other exclusive rewards.

Plus submit your purchases from now till May 30th for a chance to win a $500 Visa Card*.

Visit **HarlequinMyRewards.com** today

Earn **FREE** REWARDS Join Today! HarlequinMyRewards.com

MYR16R1